SO YOU
MAY SEE

SO YOU MAY SEE

Mona Prince

Translated by
Raphael Cohen

The American University in Cairo Press
Cairo   New York

First published in 2011 by
The American University in Cairo Press
113 Sharia Kasr el Aini, Cairo, Egypt
420 Fifth Avenue, New York, NY 10018
www.aucpress.com

Extract on pages 89–90 is from Ibrahim al-Koni's *Fitnat al-zu'an* (1995).
Reproduced by permission.

Excerpt on pages 7–8 is from "The Dedication" from *A Lover's Discourse:
Fragments* by Roland Barthes, translated by Richard Howard. Copyright © 1977
by Editions du Seuil. English translation copyright © 1979 by Farrar, Straus &
Giroux, Inc. Published in North America by Farrar, Straus & Giroux, Inc.;
reprinted by permission of Hill and Wang, a division of Farrar, Straus & Giroux,
LLC. Published in the UK by Jonathan Cape; reprinted by permission of The
Random House Group Ltd.

Dar el Kutub No. 15019/10
ISBN 978 977 416 444 6

Prince, Mona
        So You May See / Mona Prince; Translated by Raphael Cohen. —
Cairo: The American University in Cairo Press, 2011
        p.   cm.
        ISBN 978 977 416 444 6
        1. Arabic Fiction   I. Cohen, Raphael (Tr.)   II. Title
        892.73

1 2 3 4 5 6 7 8   15 14 13 12 11

Designed by Sebastian Schönenstein
Printed in Egypt

Prologue

I often said to him: I will immortalize you; I will create a myth out of you.

I will write about you and me, about our love story.

He would mock me with his words: You don't know how to write.

I teased him: Has someone loved you and written about you before? He humbly said no. My presumption would increase, and I would say: Well then, that person will be me. He would assert that I don't know how to write. I'd be quick to stifle him: You're not a literary critic, you don't even read literature. You're only interested in the news, politics, and soccer. Leave talk of writing to others.

Perhaps I don't know how to embellish my style; perhaps I don't relate to flowery language and, for that reason, refuse to use it. Whatever the case, I will still try to write this love story.

Initially, I wanted to write a novel about this love affair, but found the subject to be inconsequential. A novel about love! Could I add anything fresh to a subject already treated by great writers and philosophers? Even though I lived, and continue to live, this love with my whole being, my experience is still too limited to philosophize and theorize on the topic. In addition to this, there is the notion that a novel isn't a novel unless it deals with big issues and is leavened with ideology.

I thought, then, that love wasn't a sufficient subject to warrant the writing of a novel. So I decided to subsume it within a travel narrative. In the end the journey would be internal, a voyage of discovery or quest for some form of salvation through my physical transition from place to place; an exploration of the self and the other, the here and the there. Plus a fair amount of politics, sociology, psychology, and erotica, all of which are exciting features: a tried-and-tested recipe for fame and translation.

After I had settled on this form, I had second thoughts. I found myself rejecting all the conventional forms that I was familiar with and all the issues and subjects where I lacked experience.

I will write my love story just as it is, incomplete, and from my, sometimes less than objective, point of view. I no longer need someone to give me a voice, to adopt my perspective, or to speak on my behalf. I have a voice. I will make an effort, in accordance with my ability or my understanding, to make room for the perspective of my co-partner in the story. Let them accuse me of subjectivity and romanticism, which is no bad thing either. I will write passages based upon moments I lived through without adhering to a specific form. The passage may take the form of a narrative, a prose poem, a quotation from other texts, or a letter. A section may be long, one line, or one word; in the literary register or colloquial; with a fair deal of sarcastic asides or critical interventions that sometimes undermine what I'm writing. Well-defined form no longer concerns me. What concerns me now is to gamble at writing as I gambled at love: with even greater audacity, I will go wild with writing like I went wild with love.

Ayn

Dedication

To Ali . . .
The light by which God illuminated my heart

On Dedication

"Powerless to utter itself, powerless to speak, love nonetheless wants to proclaim itself, to exclaim, to write itself everywhere. . . . And once the amorous subject creates or puts together any kind of work at all, he is seized with a desire to dedicate it . . . .

Yet, except for the case of the Hymn, which combines the dedication and the text itself, what follows the dedication (i.e., the work itself) has little relation to this dedication. The object I give is no longer tautological (I give you what I give you), it is *interpretable*; it has a meaning (meanings) . . . ; though I write your name on my work, it is for 'them' that it has been written (the others, the readers). Hence it is by a fatality of writing itself that we cannot say of a text that it is 'amorous,' but only, at best, that it has been created 'amorously,' like a cake or an embroidered slipper. And even: less than a slipper! For the slipper has been made for your foot (your size and your pleasure); the cake has been made or selected for your taste. . . . Writing is dry, obtuse; a kind of steamroller, writing advances, indifferent, indelicate, and would kill 'father, mother, lover' rather than deviate from its fatality . . . ; there is no benevolence within writing, rather a terror: it smothers the other, who, far from perceiving the gift in it, reads there instead an assertion of mastery, of power, of pleasure, of solitude. Whence the cruel paradox of the dedication: I seek at all costs to give you what smothers you."

Roland Barthes: *A Lover's Discourse: Fragments*

1.

In Kundera's *The Unbearable Lightness of Being*, Tomas remembers that his love for Tereza was born as a result of a string of laughable coincidences: six o'clock; the novel *Anna Karenina*; a particular bench in the park, which was situated opposite the restaurant where Tereza worked; and two others that I don't recall now. He had been thinking, somewhat discontentedly and indifferently, how blind coincidences had led him to this woman who had become the love of his life, he a man who didn't believe in love and could never get enough of women.

Was it coincidence? Is there really something called coincidence, be it blind or otherwise, or is it a kind of higher arrangement, this simultaneity and succession of events that occur without us being conscious of, or even noticing, them? We just suddenly take note, think, and say, "A coincidence."

Until . . . .

A number of coincidences brought me together with that man on the first full moon of spring in the third millennium.

It was one of those Francophone parties that I know in advance will be boring. I try to cry off to the host; he doesn't accept my apologies. (I will remain indebted to his insistence that I attend.)

I go unwillingly and with no intention of staying long.

One of those parties that he knows in advance will end with the police turning up. He tries to cry off to the host; he doesn't accept his apologies. (Will he remain indebted to his friend's insistence that he attends?)

He goes unwillingly and with no intention of staying long.

I'm wearing an eye-catching Bedouin dress.

I look around. I know some of those present. Fidgety, I jiggle my leg.

As soon as he enters the party he notices my dress and asks the host if I'm Kabyle.

"I'll tell you later."

I turn to three people speaking a foreign language: a mish-mash of a local dialect, Arabic, and French. I ask the nearest person what language they are speaking.

"I'll tell you later."

I turn my face in another direction.

My desire to leave the party increases, but I'm unable to.

I pour myself a drink and go to the balcony; I look down at the street whose bustle has stilled.

A person addresses me. I turn around. It's the man I asked about his language.

A conversation begins that continues until the break of dawn.

I intend to sleep over at the host's place, but others beat me to it and the place is too crowded. Ali suggests I sleep at his place.

I go with him to his house: an apartment with three bedrooms. I can choose whichever I like. I have no desire to sleep. He asks me if I'd like some more to drink, and I say yes.

We sit talking yet more hours.

I think that was the only time Ali spoke at such length.

About nine o'clock I make coffee for both of us. I have just told him that I am going to one of the oases near Cairo to attend a mulid. He is amicably insistent that he give me a lift to the nearest place. I invite him to come with me (out of courtesy). He hesitates. Then ventures a yes.

The mulid is on the other shore of the lake. With other groups, we take a sailboat across the lake, which ends in vast desert and the tomb of Sheikh Wali.

> Both came from their own desert
> laden with historic doubts
> desolate lifeless desert
> no spring, no oasis
> we met
> we were thirsting
> at the breaking of dawn
> I asked him to kiss me
> he kissed me, kissed me, kissed
> until I was quenched
> since that kiss
> I've never been sated.

Dates come one after another, almost daily. He phones me or I phone him after he finishes work and he invites me to dinner. I pass by his office downtown, then we go together to Pub 28 in Zamalek. We drink a few Stella beers, the brand we both prefer. We have dinner, quietly conversing: the news, stories, jokes, memories.

> Something else is going on between us
> something I've not known before
> the calming tones of his voice soften the edge of my
>   inner turmoil
> his kindness and sweetness make me more tender
>   than usual
> tenderness and gentleness I didn't know I had in me
> by nature fiery, impetuous, occasionally stormy
> but something was happening
> I was lightening up
> I know I'm attractive to hotheads like me
> but this one, he's a level-headed man, very level-headed
> his words are few, precise, unadorned
> his movements also precise, understated, refined
> very refined, without affectation
> at all
> he wasn't one of those men who flaunt themselves,
> their achievements or distinctions
> he never expressed his ego in a crude, raucous way
> people might think him aloof, arrogant, or introverted
> but he's simpler than all of that
> he's a beautiful person.

I ask him to kiss me.

It's three in the morning, in his car, in the Marriot Hotel parking lot.

It's too late to go home, and I ask Ali if it's okay to stay with him.

He brings a t-shirt and shorts. I get changed. He asks me if I'd like some more to drink. I say yes. We chat a little, then . . .

It was natural for us to sleep in the same bed, some-
    thing had happened between us
a kind of familiarity, of spontaneity, that made our
    bodies' union natural
as if we'd been together in another, past life
as if our souls had been intimate since ancient times
our bodies recalled their historical union
there were no attempts to explore the other
or show off gymnastic skills
we clasp and cleave to each other, we fit
we become one being.

What does annoy me—not being used to it—is sleeping in the same bed with someone, and I can't sleep. Ali falls asleep in a minute. He wakes up a few times for no obvious reason and finds me looking at him. He's surprised and says, "Go to sleep." But I don't sleep and continue contemplating his features.

Ali's beauty isn't apparent at first glance
and not just to anyone who looks
but is discovered gradually by getting to know him
the eyes are small. He calls them two slits
the nose is big. I think it bends a little to the right.
    He denies this
the lips are full, and I'm never sated with nibbling them
the gaps between his teeth
the dimples in his cheeks that only appear when
    he laughs
from his heart.

"With you I sleep soundly."
He takes me in his arms
he wraps his left leg around my legs
and pulls me to him
he buries his nose in my hair
and starts snoring.
In the beginning I was irritated
then got used to it.
I began to feel calm when the sound filled my ears
I fold his arms around my chest
and sleep happy.

"You know I'm Nekhbet."

"Who's Nekhbet?"

"Nekhbet, the goddess of Upper Egypt who's represented in the form of an eagle."

"An eagle. So that's why you don't spend the night in your own house."

"Of course I have to fly off and see how my flock is doing. I'm a goddess."

"It's an honor."

"In another life I was a Native American."

"Really. A Native American as well."

"And I've got a Native American name, Mighty Eagle Woman. You've heard of the link between Ancient Egypt and the Native Americans? Well in either case I'm an eagle."

"Understood. But how did you know?"

"I've always felt an affinity with the Native Americans, and I can see something of them in my features. Then an Irish clairvoyant confirmed it."

"How much did you pay her!"

I laugh and finish my stories. "But my grandmother is Russian, and is proud that Abdel Nasser gave her

Egyptian citizenship after the Russians helped build the High Dam."

Ali laughs and asks, "Where did your grandfather marry her?"

"In Aswan. He was an engineer down there. They had a Nubian wedding."

He's lost in thought for a little, then asks me, "And *you* don't want to get married?"

"No. I'm a free spirit. Plus I'm a goddess, which means I'm married to the whole universe. I don't have the time."

"Amazing."

"And you, do you want to marry?"

"I don't like being tied down. But if it happens, I'll marry someone from my own country."

"Really. You mean if she's not from your country, she's no good. That you people are the only ones with women."

In this way, I make it clear to him from the outset that our sexual encounters are transient. I make him understand that I have no wish to get married and am against the idea of getting involved so that he doesn't get any ideas beyond friendship, and so that I don't get emotionally involved with him. It seems that he was also keen to get the same message across to me. We are in agreement then.

Three months later, I will ask him to get married, and he will refuse. I will ask him if I can have his baby, and he will refuse. He will ask me if I got angry at his refusal, and I will answer, "No, I guess I didn't really want to."

Spontaneously, we start to meet without prior arrangements or calls. I go by the office during the day, we order in sandwiches and eat together. Then he resumes his work, and I sit at another desk reading research papers related to my line of work. The theories tire me out, so I stop reading and look at Ali: the way his arms move when he's dealing with a fax, the tapping of his fingers on the computer keyboard, his quiet steps between the room with the news agency wires and the one with his desk.

> A hot summer breeze
> caressing not irritating
> you might not even notice
> just sense its effect on the soul
> and wonder at the secret of this sudden serenity
> and this relief that the soul does not mistake
> this breeze scintillates in your heart.

I skip over to him, sit on his knee, and kiss him on his eyes.
"What?"
"I love you."
"Just like that?"
"No, it's just that the theories are very difficult, and . . . ."
"Come on now, finish your work, don't be lazy. And let me finish my work too."
"Yes sir."
I smother his face with kisses.

My desire to be close to him grows day by day, hour by hour. The more time I spend with him in the day, the more difficult it is for me to go home in the evening. So I stay over with him at the end of the night. He senses my being torn between the longing to remain close to him and the duty to go home. He knows that my ninety-seven-year-old grandmother is waiting, although we don't know definitively for what. Sometimes she chides me for my absence, and at other times she asks me with girlish enthusiasm to let her accompany me on these late nights, which she believes are a dancing whirl of delight. This plays on his feelings, and he gives me a lift home. In front of the old house I cling to his arm and take half an hour to say goodbye. Finally, he says, "Okay, get out." He watches my soul slip from my face, and takes my hand and reassures me, "We'll see each other tomorrow."

I hug my pillow close and spend the night looking forward to the next day, until I fall asleep.

My teeth fall out while brushing. I don't lose them. But I'm horrified; losing teeth means that a person I love will die. I pick them out of the sink and decide to take them to the dentist for refitting. I calm down a little. I know that my grandmother can't die, although I don't know how this conviction has taken hold of me. Who then? Ali.

I wake up feeling anxious.

I get dressed quickly and go to see Ali at his office.

I find him well and my mind relaxes.

I make us both coffee and look over the morning newspapers.

The news is not happy reading and there's no need to recount it.

We have a political argument.

In the end, I shut him up with a kiss.

I go back to my boring theoretical readings. From time to time I look at him and see that he's absorbed in his work. I smile, because I've rarely met a person who loves his work so much. Despite the amount of time Ali spends too busy for me with the news, interviews, and conferences, I am proud of him.

He suddenly turns toward me and sees that I'm contemplating him. He gives me a long look, then resumes his work. Early on, I would ask questions, and when he didn't give a verbal response, I would look into his eyes and read them. I would read what language does not express.

I kiss his eyes.

He reminds me of a song by Abdel Wahab, "Don't kiss me on my eyes, the kissing of eyes is for goodbye."

Your eyes tempt me to kiss them with their sadness, their warmth, their depth, their mischief.

Where does this temptation lead me . . . ?

The alarm rings early in the morning. I quickly turn it off so as not to wake him up. His arms are still wrapped around me. I gently lift them and kiss his fingers.

I don't want to get up, and hesitate between going to work and staying in his arms and inhaling his breath. I kiss him on his neck, his forehead, his eyes, his fingertips. I battle with myself. He opens his eyes, "You'll be late," and kisses me. He pats me and says, "Get up." I feel like I'm dismembering myself.

I wash and dress in haste lest I miss a single moment I can remain with him.

"Have a coffee."

"It doesn't matter."

I don't want time to get lost in the making and drinking of coffee. I want to stay close to him, close to myself.

I'm conflicted between my desire to fulfill my work obligations in a job that I no longer want, and the realness of being with him.

I look at the clock, kiss him one last time, and head down before he weakens and keeps me with him.

I feel tired from staying up late, not getting enough sleep, and my hunger for him.

But I'm happy because I start my day with him.

I'm stuck. I don't know how to continue the narrative without falling into the trap of boredom.

Because this novel is in essence a novel about feelings and not action or characters—since there is only Ayn and

Ali—I now find myself confused. Despite my previous statements that I will only be writing a love story, I'm seriously worried about falling into the trap of monotony, which is a matter that the novelist, male or female, must avoid. The novel may mimic the details of real life, but it most certainly isn't bound to copy its monotony. This is perhaps where the role of the novelist comes in: to inject the novel with a shot of vivifying stimulation to prevent its descent into dullness—the literary equivalent of life's routine or a real love affair's commonplaceness. This story, despite its not lacking heated emotions and extreme reactions, is frequently difficult to represent and give expression to. Even if we were able to represent it, that on its own would not be sufficient to create a fictional world, or at least this is my belief or, more accurately, what we have grown up to believe. This being the case, it is perhaps worth my while to create some events in order to drive the narrative thread forward.

I am currently paused because I don't know what will or won't come. Let me think then of an appropriate way to draw the reader in after the previous few pages, which reveal that everything is warm and fuzzy, emotions pure, and love growing and blooming.

Let me, for example, provoke a spat. The truth is that's what really happened, as if Ayn sensed that ten pages of slush were enough. Although Ayn didn't herself feel the monotony of the relationship with Ali, and in fact was very happy up to this point, the reader may have gotten fed up with the paucity of action or suspense. I can almost feel the reader thinking, her patience largely exhausted, "Fine, but what now?"

Okay . . .

"Ayn returned from work in the afternoon and called Ali at the office. He apologized that he couldn't meet her that night because of a work crisis and promised to call her once he was done. She felt upset but didn't say so. She said to him, 'I understand.' It would be a night of reading then. She read, but without real concentration, and was forced to read each paragraph two or three times over. Between each paragraph she looked at the clock on the wall.

It had become late, and he hadn't called.

She called him on his mobile: no answer. Wasn't he done yet? She called again: he didn't answer. Was he tired? Had something bad happened to him? He doesn't want to talk to me. But nothing has happened between us to call for that. Question after question. Was he with another woman. Was it because of the work crisis? She tried calling again. The number rang unanswered. He was busy with another woman. For sure. She felt angry remembering what he had said to her on their first few dates, 'I don't like being tied down, and I love change.'

So he was with another woman. She had been surprised by her response at the time, 'I also love change.' She whiled away the whole night calling him on his mobile and at home. No answer.

She went to his office in the morning. He opened the door for her. She gave him a furious glance and stormed into his room. The following discussion ensued:

'Where were you yesterday?'

'Don't you know? I had work in the evening.'

'I called you a million times on your mobile and at home, and you didn't answer.'

'Ah, so that's why you've turned up fuming. I left it in the car and was too lazy to go down and get it. And at home you know I don't answer the phone.'

'You're a liar. You were with another woman.'

'Ayn, I don't lie to you. I told you, I forgot my phone in the car.'

'Ali, it's either me or other women.'

'Ayn, I don't like threats. I'm a free man. Do you understand?'

'Okay, you won't see me again.'

She looked at him defiantly. He looked at her in astonishment.

She left the room and slammed the door with a force that shook the high ceilings.

She met her friends in the afternoon, filled with anger. She cursed him while crying, yet not knowing why she was crying. The friends advised her to leave him: she was young and beautiful and hundreds of men would wish for someone like her. She made up her mind to do this.

But before the day was over, she changed her mind and admitted that she had provoked the quarrel, that she had gone to see him burdened with paranoid doubts that weren't necessarily true. She knew that Ali didn't lie to her. She was extremely annoyed with herself, and didn't know how to put right the wrong she had done. She was reluctant to call him lest he reject her. Her feelings that she hadn't been truthful when getting worked up with him made her ashamed of herself. She spent the whole day thinking what to do, and what his reaction would be. Finally she called.

'Can we meet?'

They met at a restaurant in Mohandiseen.

He arrived exhausted, reproving her with the eyes of a man who doesn't know how to express what he feels.

'Ayn, don't do that again. I don't lie to you.'

She didn't know where to look.

She talked about many disconnected subjects.

He listened to her in silence.

She stopped talking and looked hesitantly into his eyes.
His reproach confronted her.
Against her will, the tears welled up in her eyes.
'I'm sorry, Ali.'
They had dinner and went home together.
He enfolded her and wrapped his arms around her shoulders.
She went to sleep with a clear conscience."

Okay. So it wasn't an all-singing, all-dancing neighborhood brawl, and the reconciliation happened faster than she expected. She went back to her old ways, and even slept with a clear conscience! But I believe that the previous scene has achieved some of its stated aim, which, was it not, to cause a change in the emotional course of the narrative.

Whatever the case, this novel is not for a reader after exciting events, a depiction of society, or anything of that ilk. Ultimately, I am writing the novel that I haven't read up until now but have looked for in all the bookstores. A novel purely about love that doesn't end with Romeo and Juliet's tragic ending, nor with those terrifying happy endings where no one tells us what happens ever after.

Three months pass and I ask myself:
This Carthaginian of the mountains
what wind blew him to me
to pull up my moorings
once as fixed as ancestors in the grave
and fling me into my whirling sandstorms
what wind is it
that carried this hesitant wanderer
to a haven turned in on itself
curled up in the depths of its loneliness
awaiting a breeze to play on its windless sails

and along came an indifferent wind
recklessly scattering feathers from its mighty wings.

Toward the end of July, his words become fewer and his contemplation of me increases, like a photographer who has lost his cameras and is compelled to memorize the details of the image so they don't escape him, or as if the image will somehow vanish before he can capture it, and the splendor of the moment, which time is too mean to let reoccur, will be lost.

"I won't be coming back again, Ayn. The term of my posting has finished."

"You will be back."

"Of course I'll return to hand over the office to my successor and to get all my things."

"You'll be back and stay for another term."

"Are you a fortune-teller?"

"No. But my heart tells me you'll be back to stay."

"Your heart is mistaken, Ayn. A posting in my job lasts for three years, and may be extended for a fourth by executive decree, but that's not on the table."

"Ali, you'll stay for another term."

"What makes you so certain?"

"I haven't had enough of you yet. It's as simple as that."

The years will go by and he will come back
and I will reconfirm to him that I'll never have enough
I'll say to him that consciously or not
he drip-feeds me his beauty
doesn't pour it out in one go
so that I get filled up
and put my glass on the table with a sound that
    signals the end of the session
I'll say I receive each drop separately

and take my time savoring
till the next one comes
I'll say I was never in a rush
there is a promise between us.

He departs.

I go around in circles not knowing what to do and how
to spend this month.

I meet up with my friends again. I hear the same old
stories and the latest conspiracies and gossip. I go to the
cinema and watch comedies. I hear the audience cackling
loudly; I look into the clownish faces around me and ask
myself what they're laughing about. I attend cultural
lectures; I find myself listening to the flattery of critics who
haven't read the works of the authors they flatter.

There's nothing real.

I count the minutes until they total sixty, then strike out
an hour. I count the hours until they come to twenty-four,
then strike out a day. People complain about the day's short-
ness: I complain about its length, the slowness with which it
passes, and my helplessness.

Where are you Ali?
the whole world cannot replace you
I don't know how I'll be without you
I'll be, that's certain
but how?
I lived from the beat of your closeness
now I live on automatic
just like a washing machine
programmed according to the wash
the machine does its job
without complaining

without thinking
without feeling
since you left me.

I read a news report in *al-Ahram* announcing a change of director at the Arab Press and Media Agency. I read a news report in the London *al-Hayat* stating that the current director's appointment has been extended for another term. I telephone him to make sure. His phone is out of order. I almost go crazy waiting where I am.

I go to Mount Sinai and talk to my Lord
it's a long journey, and the ascent arduous
but I need it
I move outside myself so the inside may quiet
the further I go
the calmer my inner movement, hidden in my weary soul
the mountain, the heavens, the new moon
God and I face to face
I tell Him about Ali without shame
I know that He knows
didn't He send him to me?
I ask Him to reunite me with him
and if separation is inevitable
may it be temporary and not endure.
Two stars fall for me.
Great art Thou
Eternal on Thy throne
Small am I
I long only for Your radiant light
I come close and go far, I obey and rebel
I ask and am patient, I'm hasty and beg forgiveness
Great art Thou

I can only try to reach
and I fear the moment of union
I carry my sacrifice and make ready
I slowly ascend the mountain
and when union is near
I fall down deliberately
and start over again.

In his absence his presence becomes tyrannical.
My longing grows incandescent.
I evoke details of him and contemplate them intently.
I conjure him up,
and the habit of talking to him from afar begins.
I love him as I never loved him before
the certainty that he's the man of my life comes as
    no surprise
the man who made me a woman.
My feelings escape the fetters of the body
and soar away from me and from him.
From this distance I observe my feelings.
I watch them grow, entangle, condense
and they will pour out like rains long withheld
on ground cracked from the long wait.
Will the cracks knit and flower
or will the earth dissolve
swept away by the flood?

I'm waiting for him at the airport. The plane is an hour late.
God, isn't a month's absence enough? I pace up and down
the waiting area with my eye on the electronic Arrivals
and Departures board. His plane finally arrives. I follow the
passengers exiting from Arrivals, my patience exhausted.
Everyone has come out. Where is he?

He appears at last.

Contrary to the norm in such situations, instead of running up to him and throwing myself into his arms, I find myself rooted to the spot. He hurries toward me and takes me in his arms. I gently separate from him and feel his face and arms, his fingertips. He looks at me questioningly. "I'm making sure you've really come, and that you're still the same."

We arrive home.

I busy myself putting away travel things.

He comes to me.

I ask him where my present is.

He takes a box out of his own bag and opens it.

Antique Amazight silver jewelry which I gasp at seeing.

He waits no longer than this.

He pierces my inner being
and my longing slips away in spite of me
and my tears well up
my soul trembles as if uniting with the Holy Spirit.
My moans break and my sobbing rises
he enfolds me inside us
I willingly surrender him my soul.
I don't sleep.
He asks me what I'm thinking about.
I tell him I'm speaking to the Lord.
He's amazed
I tell him that the Lord answers my wishes when I
      ask sincerely
I add that I chastise Him when He's slow to answer
      my petition
and apologize for my haste when He does

I address Him each evening before I sleep
I thank Him if I'm with you
and ask Him that I be if I'm not
When I get tired, I ask His permission, and sleep
"And how does He answer you?"
He sends me signs
"How?"
In the coffee grinds
He falls asleep to my voice.

He loves me, and is terrified of his love for me
I love him and fear nothing
I say to him:
When I'm in your presence
I can't take my eyes off you
and when I go and lie down on the couch
that often witnesses our embraces
and close my eyes in an effort to sleep—
after a night most of which I've spent thanking the Lord
for the grace of being in your arms
and for your breath warming my neck—
my remaining senses stay alert
to your slightest movement.
Love is demanding my friend
and never satisfied
how can I explain to you
I who never bores of trying to
explain, interpret, theorize at times?
Neutral language makes me helpless.
I want to be with you
without being with you
so you're not terrified
how can that be?

Ali doesn't express his feelings, whatever they may
   be, openly.
Ayn is unlike anyone, be it man or woman, in expres-
   siveness.
For this, some might accuse her of being a dictator,
that her voice dominates the text.
So be it!
This is her text.
Plus what is she to do if the one she loves has no voice,
does not wish, a lot or little, to express himself?
Should she represent him?
Ayn isn't a proponent of representation, of what-
   ever kind:
cultural, verbal, visual.

I mentioned in the novel's prologue that I would immortalize
him by writing our love story. But now this Ali doesn't
deserve immortalizing or the glory of myth. Why? Because
he bit me on the tongue, and said he was kissing me! The
reason behind this bite, which I consider unconscious pun-
ishment, lies in the political events and big issues that I said
in the beginning I would avoid going into. I am now compelled to mention some of them as a result of that bite, or
malign kiss. A few weeks after Ali's return from vacation, the
Palestinians erupted in their third intifada. This followed
Sharon's provocative entry into al-Aqsa Mosque wearing
shoes. By coincidence this occurred on the anniversary of
Abdel Nasser's death. The upshot is a silly debate between
Ali and me where we trade accusations over Egypt's role
in current events on the Arab scene. I become enraged by
this sterile debate that forces me to defend the decisions of a
government that doesn't represent me personally. But in the
end, I don't want politics to ruin the night. I kiss him on his

mouth, and he bites me. And he doesn't let go of my tongue until the pain reduces me to tears. He looks at me in surprise and asks, "Did I hurt you?" I reply, "You're wicked."

He apologizes and says he didn't mean it and was only kissing me.

"Did it hurt you emotionally or physically?"

"I was in pain because I felt you were punishing me for something that has nothing to do with me."

He apologizes again conscientiously and stresses that he didn't mean it. I feel something else, however, for I looked into his eyes when he was biting me, and saw intention.

My child, sleeping in my arms, leaps out of bed, and his features age. I try to keep him next to me a little longer. He quickly gets up before sleep and my arms recapture him. He washes, shaves, makes coffee.

He gets dressed by himself. Today he has official engagements.

I observe him as he carefully, and by himself, puts on his tie.

He looks at me. I nod my head.

My child has grown up.

Foreign ministers, preparatory meetings, tripartite summits, quartets, twenty-member; a week passes without meeting him.

We speak on the phone.

Work, interviews, official guests.

No time for me, or for himself I think.

I pay him a flying visit at the office.

I complain to him: the office, the computer, the newspapers, the caretaker, the cigarette vendor, guests, the Arab League, the embassy, the streets of downtown, of Zamalek and Mohandiseen, the way to the airport, and more—all have a bigger share of you than I do.

He gives an exhausted smile.

I kiss his eyes and his fingertips, and move up to his mouth.

"Mmm . . . owww."

"You now realize that biting the tongue hurts?"

"You're wicked."

I look at him from above.

"Tut, tut. I'm your Lord Supreme. I'm a pharaoh, don't forget."

"My, my. You are taking advantage of the situation."

"No, I'm claiming my right."

"Oh really."

He makes a move and takes hold of me.

"Okay, okay, but no biting."

He cries off the date a number of times without any clear reason. I ask him why he's drawing away but he doesn't explain. I fail to understand and keep my distance.

He wants to be alone. I ask myself whether he's fed up with me being in his life. Does he want time to take stock of himself, his life, his plans? It's all right if he wants to separate and end the relationship, but not this gradual pulling away. I prefer a clean break. I will continue this round of love internally, in my imagination. I don't need his physical presence: I have reached the highest pitch of yearning in his absence. But I haven't passed through all the stages of love yet. Still to come are the pangs of breaking up, nostalgia, compulsion, rage, loathing, indifference, then tranquility. The circle closes and the round is over. I can conjure him up and address him, rebuke him and tease him. I can do everything. I will talk, and he will listen as usual and keep silent. This is preferable, since he doesn't have to say the words that usually frustrate me. When I yearn to hear his voice, I will summon up the few precious words that every now and again slipped out. I'll make his lips outline the

words I want to hear, like an actor in a dubbed film, and fill
in his voice in my head.

I'll summon up his fingertips and kiss them leisurely. I'll
tell him a joke and he'll laugh so that I can see the gaps
between his teeth, and I'll nibble his lower lip, and love him
more and more.

Until I exhaust all that makes love thrive and I grow
tired. I'll feel bored then and end the game.

My heart does not obey me and does not spurn him. But
I don't want to call him. I write something and send it
by fax:

> All have their messenger and their cross
> you're the one God sent to me
> as light
> to fill me inside and illuminate outside
> as a cross
> to bear my pain and witness my agony
> every prophet has his true followers
> I am your true follower
> who longs to be saturated with your light's perfume
> to cast its brilliance over the whole cosmos
> I am your true follower
> who longs to be beside, in front of, behind, you
> not to bound you, as you'll understand it
> but to obey your words when you're right
> to guide your steps when you're lost
> to support you when you're weary
> to light your heart when it darkens
> like your light illumined her soul before
> but you're a mad prophet
> a prophet who rejects his prophecy.

One of my girlfriends diagnosed my condition: I'm not sufficiently 'ladylike.' That is, I lack that feminine sense that knows how to pursue a man and make him traipse panting behind her. I say to her that I'm not out hunting for a man, that I love a human being. She says, "But you have to make him feel that you're busy, that you have other interests, that you don't always have enough time to be with him." I reply that I don't know how to pretend to be something I'm not, and that I couldn't be a true lover if I were too busy for him. I say to her, "How can I feel that he wants to be with me and say I'm sorry, I'm too busy?" She says, "God, you're an idiot." Perhaps.

Ali and I meet later on.

"I'm going to say something to you that perhaps I shouldn't."

He looks at me questioningly and in surprise. He's used to my saying what I have to say without introductions. I tell him my friend's advice. He laughs as though I'd cracked a joke.

"What?"

"Why don't you try."

"What! Really, you want me to act with you like that!"

I phone my friend and tell her what happened. "Didn't I tell you you're an idiot?"

"Yes I believe so!"

Another friend has read the above and considers that it doesn't attain the status of a 'novel': the text up until now lacks plot and does not develop and, in the best case, is a long short story or, if the narrative parts are eliminated, a particular poetic state. A third friend thought that the text was suspended in a void since it lacks perspective and is disconnected from reality. Now, although I don't know how I will continue the narrative, I still want to write this text—

forget about novel—without encumbering it with extraneous matters. Perhaps I am not able to write a novel in the conventional sense of the term, that is to create a more or less self-contained structure which conveys a certain vision (whole, partial, fragmented, etc.) of the world.

I could indicate to the reader—if this will be of benefit—the general context in which these two characters live. I could also give some personal information about the two characters, if that will make them tangible personalities.

So, the novel's action occurs, sorry, the characters in this text first appear in Egypt in the year 2000 and continue up to the moment of writing. They may continue for longer than this (God knows best). The contemporary reader is aware of the political, social, and economic events pertaining to this period, and to which I truly hate even alluding. The non-contemporary reader—if such exists—will have to turn to the newspapers of the period if they so desire.

As I have already mentioned, the only protagonists are Ayn and Ali. Ayn is a woman, around middle age, with very Egyptian features, ever proud of being a descendant of the pharaohs, and a social researcher who sees no value in her research. She wants to love.

Ali is a man past middle age, from a 'sister' Arab state, of Berber ancestry, and posted to work in the press and media in Egypt. Until this moment he does not know what he wants. He takes each day as it comes.

Is this sufficient? I don't know.

Whatever the case, I will continue writing as seems fit to me. If I don't succeed in writing a gripping narrative, may the reader forgive me. In that case, I will rewrite in a form closer to an extended free verse poem.

Let's see how things go!

Then I turn my back and try to warm myself up by wrapping the blanket around my body. But my back is still cold because I can't cover it. He is lying next to me.

Everything is really cold: the bed, the sheets, the cover. Only his body is warm. He tries to warm me up and his hands and legs get cold. We lie still a while. I'm thinking about him and looking at him next to me.

"What are you thinking, Ali?"

"About loads of things."

I grow angry. I wait. He doesn't add a word.

We are lying on our backs. He puts his hand over his eyes to shield the light coming into the room from the street. I stare blankly at the ceiling.

"What?"

A minute or more passes by before I answer, nothing. I feel colder than before.

He doesn't take me in his arms as he used to. He turns his back to me.

I feel suffocated, confined. I am trying all the time to slip out of his arms, and he won't let me. Little by little, I have gotten used to resting my head on his right arm and to his wraping his left arm around me and clasping his hands together on my chest. I have begun to feel warmth, love, acceptance, that I am part of him, and he part of me.

Why doesn't he try to caress me?

I want to get out of the bed. I can't bear his back against me. I don't want to be next to him.

I feel a desire to smoke. I get up. I turn on the television and light a cigarette. He asks me for a cigarette. I light it for him and sit watching a boring TV discussion while he smokes his cigarette without speaking.

Maybe I can sleep in the spare room. But I know he doesn't like to wake up and not find me next to him. But what about me? Why am I forced to remain in the same bed now that I can't stand him?

I go unwillingly back to the bed. He isn't asleep.

I try to sleep, to think about what I have to do the next day. I have to do this and I have to do that but he gets in the way of everything. He's distracting me from all the things I have to do. I get angry. I roll over in the bed. One, two, three, four . . . sleep doesn't come to me and neither does he. After a while he lights another cigarette. I turn toward him. He knows that I'm annoyed by the smell of the smoke in bed. He gets up and takes the packet with him to the kitchen.

I'm worried about him being cold. Why doesn't he take me in his arms? Why doesn't he try? I would refuse once, twice, three times, but in the end I'd accept him. Why doesn't he just try?

Why all this distance?

I lose interest. Let him go to the kitchen, let him go to Hell, let him burn, let him freeze, let him disappear. I don't care.

I begin to feel tired from talking to myself, from trying to sleep, and from trying to evade the sensation of lying next to him. In the end I fall asleep.

He wakes up before me in the morning. I sense him but pretend to sleep.

He washes, shaves, and goes into the kitchen to make coffee.

He stands in front of me and calls me by my name. I open my eyes.

"Good morning."

"Good morning." I respond with all the sorrow in the world.

We sit in silence sipping coffee and smoking morning cigarettes.

"Did you sleep well?"

"Yes. Did you sleep well?"

"Yes."

We're lying to each other and we're not used to lying.

I no longer have any desire to speak. I no longer have any desire to tell him about my pain.

He doesn't understand. Or perhaps he does, but can't, can't give himself over to the state of being in love, the obsession of loving, the love of loving.

I yearn for my yearning for him, for my pangs for him when he's present and when he's absent. He just loves me. He's not interested in passion. He's not interested in the detail.

I ask him what he feels when I tell him I love him. He responds that it makes no difference whether I say it or not because he knows that I love him. But don't you feel something different, more happiness, another sensation? I try to make him understand that I want him to say it, I want my ears to enjoy its resonance. "It's got the effect of magic, try and understand."

I look at his chin, he hasn't cut it shaving as usual. He stands up to get dressed. I stand up to get dressed. Then I sit on the arm of the chair looking at the floor and waiting for him to finish gathering up his things.

He lifts my head toward him and gives me three quick kisses.

I look at him and away from him, into his eyes and behind his eyes.

He distances himself.

Ayn strives for love

Ali flees from love

how is it possible to combine these two opposite characters?

Ayn makes some suggestions:

1. To love him for life

2. To love him for a year, with the option to renew
3. To love him until she meets someone else
4. To love him part-time
5. To love him in ten years' time

She asks him which he'd like to choose.

He takes his bedding to the spare room.

She notices a smile on his face. She goes after him.

"Fine. Would you like me to hate you?"

He finally laughs and says yes.

"Okay, just not this room please, it feels like a torture chamber."

They return to the bed on the floor in the liv-ing room.

He started avoiding me.

Every time we do meet, we go around the same vicious circle of questions and wordless accusations that invariably ends with us sleeping in separate rooms.

Conversation begins amiably on my side and he is responsive.

Suddenly the same devilish questions leap to my mind. I close my eyes and try to silence them, but they appear in different guises. I roll onto his chest and kiss him; he takes me in his arms. I dismiss evil thoughts, they evade me for a while, then come back, surround me, fill my head with noise, make my chest hurt with sighs, and drive away my ardent desire for him.

I submit. The questions declare themselves victorious, declare themselves. That's what they want, then. They're not interested in the answers, which they know in advance, having heard them time and again. What do these ques-tions want from me? They want to interpose themselves between me and him, they want each of us to make the other angry, to open up a space of dismay between us. I explain to him what's happening to me, and ask for his help so that the questions don't win. He thinks it best not to answer them.

I'm annoyed. Perhaps the questions aren't interested in the answers, but I want to hear them, and begin:

"Why?"

"Because you know all the answers. You're just pretending to be blind to them."

"Blind to what?"

His eyes beg me to stop interrogating him.

"Do you prefer love or freedom?"

"I told you before that I can't bear being tied down, that I don't like anyone to hold me to account, that freedom is the most important thing in my life."

"That's what you said before you loved me. I am asking about now."

"I haven't changed my opinion. I don't change. Try and understand."

"What do you mean you haven't changed. How come love hasn't changed you, but I have changed?"

"I'm not you. You asked me for my opinion and I gave you an honest answer. Why are you angry now?"

"I'm not angry, I'm astonished."

"Be astonished, that's your business."

I get angry. I feel I've been insulted. I search his eyes for an answer that I'm happy with; he closes his eyes and withdraws.

I go into the spare room crying. Why is he treating me like this? Why does he ignore me, why doesn't he have feelings for me? Because he doesn't love me as much as I love him. Because he doesn't want me as much as I want him. I will leave him. Tomorrow, I will leave him. I won't see him again. He doesn't deserve me. But I love him. I'll leave him for a while. I won't phone him. I won't go by the office. I'll travel. I'll get to know someone else. I'll leave him until he longs for me. It goes on like this until I get tired and fall asleep.

She enters a rundown bar in a small town off the map
sets a vague face that suits the town's sprawl of slums
checks out the bar with a neutral gaze
sits in a far dark corner
asks for a glass of red wine and lights a cigarette
crosses her legs revealing her thighs
a conceited young man steps toward her
he comes closer raising his glass
she blows smoke in his face and turns away
she's not impressed by her performance and
checks out the bar again with a gaze that says, look-
    ing for a good time
she finds him in another corner
on his own drinking a glass of red wine
she picks up her glass and goes over
sits down next to him
and crosses her legs revealing her thighs
he gives her a presumptuous look
which she knows well
she winks her left eye and smiles a come-on
before she sheds a tear from the same eye and the
    smile frowns
she chats in a foreign language he barely knows
but he listens
and at the end of the night he takes her with him
and in bed she measures his fingers
and looks for the gaps between his teeth
she lets him toy with her a little then gets up
I'm sorry: you're only a little bit like him
a very little bit.

I awake to his calling out. I heard him calling me, imploring.
I go over to him and find him asleep and breathing with a
pained sound. How come, when I've just heard his voice very
clearly. I remember that I said I would leave him, but doesn't
this calling out mean he wants me to stay?

I debate with myself until I reach the same conclusion.

I suppress my anger, ignore my desires, and play tricks
on myself so that the anger between us doesn't increase.

I go to his bed. He holds me to him.

I'm delighted, really delighted. I fall asleep.

We wake up exhausted.

I see his weary features.

I feel guilty and apologize and promise it won't happen
again.

I was making soup in an aluminum pan on a high heat
the water boils off and the consistency thickens
I found myself thinking that things are like that
happiness evaporates and pain sticks
and if you left the soup on the heat—high or low—
for longer
and endured the pain, allowing time to cool it
it would burn, and its remnants would stick more
    and more to the bottom
and its blackened residues would never be erased
unless you made heroic efforts
like scrubbing the bottom of the pan with wire wool
made from the same metal as the pan, with all your
    strength
or you got rid of the pot completely
by giving it to the junkman together with a fair quantity
of old newspapers, in exchange for a plastic plate for
    example.

But if you were using a non-stick pan
you'd only have to add a few drops of washing-up
     liquid
plus a little water.
Put the pan on the heat for a few minutes
and the pan will be just as before, or perhaps better.
But you should be aware
if you're inattentive, the pan will get burnt again
and with repeated burning non-stick loses its char-
     acteristic
and becomes like the aluminum pan with blackened
     residues.

What's the problem? What's the problem?

Why does our relationship swing from one extreme to another? One minute we're very happy, and in the next the world's turned upside down, and we've become like the Israelis and Palestinians, one of us trying to exterminate the other.

We get dismayed with each other, but I don't have the strength to keep away, waiting for him to initiate a reconciliation. So I go and see him. For days at a time I expend superhuman nervous energy to shift anger out of our way. Making up with him exhausts me when he's being impossible. But I love him being impossible.

I love him for his tenderness. And there is tyranny in his tenderness.

His accusation against me is that we keep going round the same circle, never making progress.

Yes, because you've put barriers in the middle of the road and said that these are your boundaries, which you'll never go beyond. Whenever I move forward I bump into a barrier and go back to the beginning. It's you who's blocking my progress. It's you who's shutting the doors and me who's always trying to open them.

He denies this. He says he's never been with a woman in the way he is now with me.

The truth in his eyes and the tone of his voice make me believe him.

But there is something that makes him, makes him, I don't know exactly, distant perhaps.

I ask myself why this relationship doesn't develop. Why togetherness then separation? Why this strange mutual desire to end the relationship and the lack of any true capability to do so? The relationship comprises two parties. Even if I can control myself, I can't control the other party or his personality or make up. My self surprises me: You mean why can't you keep him. I reply to myself as though I'd caught my self out. Ahh, that's it then, keeping him, possession. You want to keep him for yourself and he wants to keep himself for himself. Herein lies the conflict. How is it possible to possess someone who doesn't want to be possessed. The problem then is in my ability. I feel disappointed because I'm incapable, that is I can't do something I want to. I'm the problem. Me.

I go and see the Irish clairvoyant and ask her to invoke the spirit of Ali's father. Fanny says this is an extremely difficult proposition in the absence of Ali. She requests that Ali come in person. I tell her that he'll never come. For, in addition to not believing in such things, he doesn't care to know the future and prefers events to take their course without meddling on his part. She asks me what I want from his father. Advice perhaps. He knows his son well. What I should do to make the relationship work. Fanny tries to summon his father's spirit and engage him in conversation. But she lets me know from the beginning how difficult this is and that she's not certain of the outcome.

In some way she makes him present. She gives a description and says a name. "That's his name," I say, "Abdel Qadir." I take out the old photograph of Ali as a small child with his father and siblings. I inspect the image of the father and compare it with Fanny's description of the form she has invoked. "Yes, it seems to be him."

"It seems he was one of the rebels who fought the war against the French." Fanny's voice comes from very far away and her eyes are closed, as though she were in a distant land, even though she is sitting right in front of me.

"He really was like that, according to Ali. He insisted on sending his son, who wasn't even a teenager, to a city far from their village to learn Arabic. The French had banned the teaching of Arabic at that time, and the father saw it as a form of resistance and as an act of faith in the Arab identity of his country."

Fanny makes a huge effort to get Abdel Qadir's spirit to speak, but he doesn't. She shakes her head. "His mouth is shut tight. He seems to be a conservative character and not the talkative kind." She could have been describing Ali. He's like his father then.

I inspect anew the black-and-white photograph that I picked up surreptitiously from Ali's desk drawer. He told me that the picture had been taken for them before he left the village for the city. He was crying, clinging on to the jallabiya of his mother who didn't want her son to be far away from her. But the father, the revolutionary, was very determined, which was also apparent in the photo. Ali took the photograph with him to every country he visited. He grew used to traveling as a child. Perhaps that's what makes him unable to settle down and form long-term relationships, and so his relationships were always transient. I smile as I remember Ali saying that his relationships usually lasted three months, possibly extending to six months. I also remember how I shouted in his face, "Are you renting a flat with an option to renew!" and how Ali laughed at the comparison, which perhaps contained an element of truth. More bizarrely, he only formed relationships with foreign women who spoke good English, of which he knew only a few words, and that didn't speak French, in which he was fluent. "How do you communicate then?" I asked him once. "We don't talk much. We use primitive signs." That's what he's like. Because he's always traveling, he's worried about involvement and its consequences. Maybe.

Fanny opens her eyes, and returns from her visionary journey. "The only thing I can say to you is that you're in a relationship with a very difficult person."

My teeth fall out for the second time in the space of few months. I'm horrified when I see my mouth, toothless, in the mirror. I put them in again, but not in the original arrangement. My mouth is no longer the way it was. When I chew my food I feel severe pain, even if the food is soft.

I tell myself I have to reach a decision. But what decision?

I will make him choose whether to be with me or not be with me.

Is this a new question? No.

I put on a dress whose colors are like spring and the silver jewelry he gave me.

I go and see him at the office. He greets me warmly. I look at him dubiously.

He asks me why I'm wearing the earrings and bracelet but not the necklace.

I touch my neck and don't find the necklace. But I put it on. I'm certain.

"Perhaps you lost it on the way."

"I'll go and look for it."

"You won't find it. There's no point looking. I'll bring you another one next vacation."

I tell him the dream of the teeth. He says hallucinations.

We go to La Chesa's on Adli Street. We order beer and a snack.

I don't feel like eating or drinking.

"I'll get you another one."

"Losing your first present is a bad omen. To me it means I'm going to lose you or the relationship will end."

"No superstitious nonsense please."

"I'm going to look for it in the places I was."

"Don't tire yourself out. You won't find it."

"I will find it."

I come back half an hour later thinking about the meaning of signs.

I sit opposite him and contemplate him.

"I told you, you wouldn't find it."

I put it on the table in front of him.

"Here it is, just damaged. I found it in the street."

"Don't be upset. I'll buy you another one."

"Something is going to damage our relationship."

He screams in his sleep next to me. I wake up and look at his face. He looks like someone struggling with phantoms or trying to get free of some grip and failing. I don't know whether to wake him up or leave him to break his silence.

In the morning I ask him why he was screaming. He looks at me in surprise and answers the question with a question, "Did I scream?"

"Yes."

"Did I say anything?"

"You were letting out disjointed sounds, like words but not clear."

"Perhaps it was nightmares."

"Should I wake you up if you scream again?"

"No, leave me to scream."

The screaming reoccurs on a number of nights. I ask myself whether he no longer slept soundly with me in the way he had told me in the beginning. A man sleeps soundly next to the woman he loves. Isn't it like that, Kundera? Has Ali lost his love for me? Why do I think of it as a 'loss'? Is it not possible that it means relief for him. The loss is mine, if I want. But why complicate things. Why isn't it just nightmares or some problems? Some problems. I think about nothing but problems.

He hasn't been honest with me.
I came to know from a mutual friend from his country.
The news hit me like a hammer blow.
But I didn't scream with pain.
I was just stunned.
By coincidence—or ironically—
I was picking up a present from a jeweler's near
    his office,
where I had placed a special order.
I left confused.
I don't know what to do with the present.
It has become meaningless, without occasion.
True there is an occasion!
I climb the staircases of the old building
and before knocking on the door
I look at my face in the mirror in the corridor.
My features are comatose.
That's better!

Because what ought to be marked on my face now?
anger, sadness, pain, hatred.
But I don't feel anything definite.
The dissonance between the news and picking up
    the present
has made my mood closer to sarcastic than anything
    else.

The question has become
what will his reaction be when he knows that I know
and with the knowledge, a gift!
I knock on the door
he opens in greeting and kisses me on the cheek as usual
we sit down
we look at each other expectantly
he's waiting for me to start talking
and I find nothing to say.
I offer the present
he asks what it is
a gold chain with an inscribed pendant
I read it to him:
"His nose slips into the curls of my wavy hair
breathing in my fragrance scented with henna
in the morning I feel my hair
and find it moist with the fitful vapor of the night
clumped and messed up."
He gives a questioning glance.
I'm forced to interpret.
I wanted to give you something meaningful to both
    of us
the nose is your nose; the hair is my hair
you are breathing; the air is my air.
He doesn't understand.

Never mind.
He puts it round his neck.
You're not obliged to wear it,
I say
and go out without our broaching the subject.

My writing is blocked again, in the same way that Ayn's emotions have become blocked following her last meeting with Ali. For months, I'm cut off from writing in the same way that Ayn is cut off from Ali and from herself. My block, which meant being unable to write, was the result of regional political events. At that time it was not possible—so I believed—to complete my ravings about love while war was raging next door. However, after my unlamented withdrawal from the political scene —having realized its absurdity and becoming certain that the big issues were illusions—it became clear to me that what I had considered to be ranting was more real than anything else

Language slips away from me and I have stopped both writing and reading. Only the all too frequently misleading language of the news channels comes to mind.

I miss Ayn, her language, and her feelings.

I reread what I have written and imagine her from a distance. How would she overcome the block preventing her from resuming the narrative after all this distance. Perhaps like this:

To compose one line of these pieces
I have to recollect many
moments of absolute joy
hours of convulsive pain
days of fixed sadness
nights of mordant longing

months of waiting and fear of loss
years bearing the remains of a memory
eroded by the action of aging.

Perhaps.

Severing.
That's the solution.
I go to a remote desert wadi in Sinai. I want to get as far
away as possible.
He calls repeatedly, and I don't answer the phone. I have
nothing to say. What can I say to an engaged man preparing
to get married? I try to convince myself that I'm strong. I
repress all my feelings and deal only with the decision to
amputate. I walk back and forth along the wadi. I'm a free
woman; he's a free man too, my self answers me. Why the
anger then? I'm not angry. He said that when he got married,
it would be to a woman from his own country. True, but he
didn't say he would do it behind my back. Did you want him
to tell you from the beginning that he had gotten engaged
and lose you? In that case he wants to keep hold of me without
losing the other woman. I feel disgust. How could we spend
most of our time together, eat together, drink together, go to
bed and wake up together, while he's making arrangements
for his marriage to another woman? So he doesn't love me?
He's amusing himself; he's spending time with me until he
goes home to his country and marries this woman. But he
loves me. I'm certain that he loves me. But how can he love
me and marry another? You mean you wanted him to
arrange his wedding with you then? Of course not, I don't
want to marry him. What do you want then? I get angry with
my self and shut her up.
Yet the question won't leave me alone. What do I want?

I remember my teeth that fell out and his screaming when asleep next to me.

I'm in pain. I want to be with him. But I'll never be with him. I've made up my mind. I hate him because he pushed me into this decision.

I cry. Why are you crying, Ayn? I miss him.

I remove my shoes and speak to my Lord:

O Lord, I don't know whether to thank You or
    blame You
should I thank You for the love You have given me
or blame You for the beloved who runs away from love?
O Lord, if You know my condition
I who crave love
and he who flees love
why did You join us?
O Lord, I have believed You and praised You greatly
You tempted me
so why deprive me now?
or are You testing me?
O Lord, You granted him the power to control his
    feelings
and granted me only the power to love
and it's become out of place.
What's the rationale?
If separation is inevitable, let it be temporary and
    not be long
if there is no good in this love, may You turn my
    heart from it
and forgive Yourself, O Lord.

I lie down on a small patch of grass and look up at the sky. I start counting the numberless stars until I fall asleep.

A black clot is blocking my left nostril and obstructing my breathing.

It suddenly dislodges and flies out. I open the door of the room for it.

My window is wide open and a white bird enters.

It leaves me some of its feathers and resumes its soaring.

I breathe.

I awake at dawn feeling serene. I feel my left nostril. I'm well.

I think about the dream. What's holding me back? My feelings or my thoughts?

What do I feel? Contentment. What else? Love.

I fly into Cairo and touchdown at his house. He gives me a look filled with everything I felt in Sinai. We embrace and resume what was severed.

"Why did you leave? And why have you come back?"

"I don't know why I left, but I do know why I'm back."

"Why?"

"I've come to make up with my self."

No woman revealed to you so much of herself as me.

How can I not, for the self hides nothing from the self.

Me as well, Ayn, I've never been with a woman like
      I am with you.

I've never entrusted my soul to anyone as I have
      to you.

Shyly, his eyes speak a deep love.

His lips whisper as though fearful of what they
      might divulge.

I take him in my arms and kiss his brow and eyes.

Why then:

"If I were to ask you to marry me, say no."

"Ali . . ."

"Change the subject please."

I insist . . . .

He slips gently out of my arms.

He lies down on the couch. He closes his eyes. He withdraws.

I go into the kitchen. In tears I scoff all the food he has cooked for us, leaving him nothing. I gulp down three large whiskies and go into the spare room. I curl up in a cold bed. My stomach is upset. I go to the bathroom and throw up my pain.

Ali comes after me. He stands with me until I'm done, then looks at me reproachfully.

He takes me by the hand to our bed on the floor. We lie down on our backs.

"Ali. I ate all the food."

"Yes, then you threw it up."

"Did you have your eye on it?"

I feel his smile in the dark.

"You're not hungry are you? I can make you something else. There's some cheese in the fridge."

"No. It's okay. I'm going to sleep. You should sleep too."

"Are you sure?"

"Sure."

He pulls the sheet over us.

He buries his nose in my hair, clasps his arms around my chest and starts to breathe deeply.

To be on the border
not here or there
but wishing to be here and there
in the middle ground
that thorny place
what can you do?

will you carry your suitcases and cross the border to
    what's there
or head back to what's here?
what's here sheer joy
for me and you perhaps
here too stands for us—too
there you are happy alone
with no me or us
maybe you prefer to stay on the border
in between, neither here nor there
excusing yourself the onus of making up your mind.
Perhaps the border will fall all by itself
and make you completely free, completely set free.

In *The Unbearable Lightness of Being*, Kundera reflects
on the idea of lightness/heaviness. He states that while we
are crushed by the heaviest burdens, the literature of love
affirms woman's desire to be weighed down by the man's
body. Thus at the same time, the most crushing burden also
represents the ultimate culmination of desire. The more we
are pushed down toward the ground, the truer our lives. Yet
without any burdens man becomes weightless and floats
free. No longer bound to the earth he loses his reality and
his actions lose their meaning.

    What will you choose? Weight or lightness?
    What will you choose Ali?

I don't know how to deal with his indecision. I just don't know.
I back him into a corner and ask him to answer honestly. He
says he doesn't know. His indecisiveness freaks me out. Without meaning to, I start to make problems everywhere, in the
office, at home, in bars, in the street. He keeps his distance,
I break down, and go back in tears. He has no patience for

my weakness or his, and his eyes beg me to stop torturing him and torturing myself.

> I will train my ever-excitable self
> to smile gently even in the direst circumstances
> just like the Japanese when overcome
> by anger, worry, or grief.
> I will smile to seem nice to him
> like a sweet delicacy on display
> tempting those looking while waiting for someone to
>   pay the price of a taste
> yet resigned to the voiding of what the stomach
>   cannot take
> out of a single outlet together with other waste.
> I will smile because when I looked at my face in the
>   mirror
> as I cried, I was annoyed by my looks.
> I will smile and mumble a few meaningless words
> which he mostly won't hear, and won't understand
> that when I peer inside from the edge of myself
> I find an ever deepening circular void
> that deliberately, meticulously, hollows out my lone-
>   liness
> I panic, get confused, and commit what he calls folly.
> I will smile in front of you the smile of a nice refined
>   girl.
> I will cling to this lesser loneliness
> so as not to slip over the edge.

I settle my grandmother down in her favorite seat. I prepare us both a glass of her special Russian brew, which her brother distills at home in the Russian countryside. I imagine that she is looking at me, although in fact I don't know whether she can actually see or not. Her eyes are always open since, in some fashion and over time, her eyelids have disappeared without anyone noticing. She never talks about the subject. We can only tell she's asleep from the sound of her snoring.

I hand her the glass. In propitiation to her, we drink a toast to the health and memory of Abdel Nasser.

I tell her what the deal is. She seems to be listening. But I'm not sure. I ask her what I should do. She shakes her head with a kind of sorrow. I ask her which of us is wrong. She shakes her head again. I pour her another drink, perhaps this will help her collect her thoughts. Inspiration strikes in Russian.

"Nana, I don't understand a word. Speak Arabic."

I'm forced to consult the dictionary. Roughly, she means that there's no benefit in the relationship, and that I'm wasting my time. I tell her that I love him and want to be with him. She is silent for so long, I suspect she's fallen asleep. "Nana." She replies in her language. I reopen the dictionary.

"What?"

I laugh loudly and am unable to stop. I don't believe what my grandmother is saying. "Bewitch him."

"What do you mean, 'Bewitch him'? Nana, are you serious?"

I'm suddenly aware of the sound of her snoring. I laugh involuntarily and take the empty glass out of her hand. I lead her to bed and wish her, "Sleep well and sweet dreams." She responds with a musical snore.

"Bewitch him."

Despite its weirdness, the idea sparks inside me.

Through some acquaintances, I made contact with one of those sheikhs who use magic and charms, and of whom it is said, 'he works wonders.' I go and see him at his house in a neighborhood of Old Cairo. The man, whom I thought would be very old, turns out to be less than thirty. He's wearing very ordinary clothes that don't hint at magic. Or at least not in the way I imagined or we see in films. For a while I thought he might be a conman and wanted to back out. But the man doesn't give me the chance to escape. He orders me to sit down on the mud floor, and lights various kinds of incense. Fear grips me. He asks me what kind of spell I want. I tell him a love spell. He asks for a photograph capturing both me and the person for whom the spell is desired and something that smells of him. I ask him how to perform the spell. He replies in vague terms. All I understand is that he will harness one of the benevolent jinn and use him to influence the man I love and make him infatuated with me. I tell him straightaway that I don't want him infatuated, I just want him not to stay away.

We agree on another appointment the following week once I have assembled the photograph and something of his.

The photo is a cinch, but something of his? How can I pinch a piece of smelly underwear?

I start thinking about the subject. Am I really serious or just playing around? Part of me believes in the jinn, another part isn't convinced, part is looking for adventure, and part is scared of the consequences. What if I went down this path and didn't know how to get back? What if I was changed and didn't know myself? What if Ali was harmed in some way, or his personality changed and he became a different person, a stranger to me? What if the spell was too strong, and Ali became seriously infatuated and started following me like my shadow or trailing behind me with wild hair like a mad beggar? What if I wasn't happy with the spell, how would I break it?

I conclude that the subject is too big for me and it's better not to play with such things.

If Ali doesn't want to be with me of his own free will, I won't make him stay with magic and won't beg him.

On the way to his office, my eyes alight on a book of magic in the middle of a pile of old secondhand books. I hesitate for a second then pick up the book and brush off the dust, *The Harnessing of Demons in the Unification of Lovers*. I look for the index. Not there, nor is there a table of contents. The seller, at the end of his patience, asks whether I am buying the book or will read it for free while standing there. I pay up and go to a café near Ali's office. I order tea and sit leafing through the pages. I come across crude geometrical drawings done by hand, chapter headings for various spells, including a love spell, and contiguous letters that don't spell out any recognizable words. Under the title of Love, I find a list of instructions, one of which is impossible: the repetition of a particular charm one thousand times. The idea is that the continuous repetition of certain sounds will have an effect and bring about the desired result. But how to reach the thousandth time without miscounting? I drink the tea and go to see Ali.

He welcomes me with great affection. I burst out laughing. I say to myself that the spell that I didn't work has worked. He asks me why I'm laughing. A new fit of laughter begins. He leaves me and resumes his work. I finally come round from the fit of laughter.

I take the book out of my bag and sit on his knee. I read him the love spell that is to be written on an egg laid on a Saturday. He starts to laugh incessantly. When I reach the charm that must be repeated one thousand times over a sugar lump, to be blown on three times after every count of ten,

"Malkish balkish shasha kashka mahyush galgamish," he says through his laughter, "If you say that charm a thousand times, I'll give you a thousand pounds." Then I tell him about my visits to the man who prepares spells. He shakes his head and says, "You're crazy. Why do you want to do this?"

"To keep you with me."

"Well, we're together."

"Okay. So that you love me as much as I love you."

"Well I love you, and you know that."

"Really? Okay, why do you love me?"

"For your honesty, your innocence, your spontaneity, and your madness. I've never seen them in another woman."

The nightmare question almost slips out of my mouth, and I bite my tongue by mistake. He notices the question on my face and laughs. He comments on my biting my tongue, "No doubt you were going to ask a dumb question."

"Yeah!" We laugh together. Then he takes my tongue into his mouth for a long dreamy kiss.

"You taste really good, Ali."

"Really?"

"I want to eat you up."

"Eat!"

I scratch him, kiss him, bite him. He gets turned on and does likewise.

I read *The Alchemist* by Paolo Coelho and am arrested by the idea that if you truly want something, this desire originates in the soul of the world, and the universe as a whole conspires to make it real. I believe in all creations, the living and the inanimate, the visible and the invisible. Each of us carries inside and embodies the soul of the world. When I wish for something, I wish for it from the whole universe. But is that enough to make what I wish come true? I am confused between my power to act which comes from God and my destined fate, which too comes from God. Is it possible to alter the predestined course? But I also don't know what is decreed or how things will end up. I am on the path, and I believe I will only know this at its end, which also means my end, or at least the end of this form of life.

It's New Year in a few days. I ask Ali where he'd like to celebrate.

"We won't spend it together."

"Why? Are you going away?"

He looks at me, apprehensive of my response. Then he says impassively, "My fiancée is coming."

I remember that there is another woman, whose identity is unknown to me, and to whom in some way I have become oblivious. But this doesn't prevent me from asking him in astonishment, and condemnation too, "Why?"

"She wants to see me."

I still don't understand and persist, "Why?"

Ali smiles in the face of my astonishment.

"Ayn, she's my fiancée and wants to see me. Should I say no?"

"Yes, say no to her. Tell her you're busy."

"I can't."

"Well then, say it's you who wants to see her."

He turns his head away.

"You won't see her Ali."

"How come? Will you stop me?" he asks, furious.

"I won't let her come."

He laughs disdainfully. "What, will you cast a spell on her!"

I also laugh and answer with the defiance of a sorceress, "I tell you she won't come, you'll see. And I'll tell you something else: you won't marry her."

We don't talk about the subject again.

One day before the end of the year, Ali calls and asks where I'd like to spend New Year.

I am the one who made you a prophet
but never forget
I'm the goddess
I chose you unto yourself
and you chose to submit to another
keep away as you wish
but the choice is not yours
because you're linked to me with an umbilical cord
go
I know how to pull you back
you'll never really go
except when the term is over
and I cut the cord
show a little patience
your due time will come.

With the onset of summer and the approach of his vacation, the rhythm of distance and closeness, which has
become characteristic of this relationship, increases in
intensity. My level of anxiety rises in turn, as does my
inability to act.

Anger accumulates and mounts within me
I pounce on intentional and unintentional mistakes
I wait for chances
and at the point of explosion
I shut my eyes and hold my breath
I fade away
this is better, I say to myself
and in my imagination I create fights however I like
for example four of us having dinner
three of us from the same country
and me from another

the trio speak in their language
and I don't understand
I drop a hint
he says: things that don't concern you
and resumes his conversation
I imagine my response:
I leap to my feet and say:
don't invite me again to a gathering
where you speak about things that don't concern me
and I leave the place in a huff
or
I stand up calmly and tell him
I'm going to sit with other people
who are talking about things that might not concern me
but in a language I understand
then I examine my two reactions:
the first will anger him, but he might take my hand
and switch the conversation to other things in a com-
	mon language
and I sit down on edge
the second will wound him, and he might not for-
	give me
and I'm afraid I'll lose him
and miss another opportunity to end a relationship
we've been trying to end since it began.

For many years, a woman with one leg has been visiting in the
summer. Every day before sunrise, she leans on her metal stick
and walks between my house and the Bedouin Moon Beach,
her eyes fixed on some point inside her. On the night of the full
moon she walks the few feet from my house to the edge of the
coral reef. She puts her stick to one side and sits cross-legged,
her good leg over the half-amputated one. She looks ahead at

the shy ascent of the orange full moon from behind the distant mountains. Once the moon is high in the sky and its orange glow turns silver, the woman stands up, supporting herself with her stick, and returns to the house. This time, at moonrise, the woman wasn't sitting as usual. She was standing on her one good leg without a stick, her eyes fixed on the same inner spot. Once the orange pathway was laid before her and touched the toes of her one leg, she bent her leg and launched her whole body into the pathway. From my window there was only a metal stick gleaming on the edge of the water and the moon continuing its calm ascent into a sky whose stars had vanished.

I feel my soul returning to my body at the end of its nocturnal wanderings. I come round from the stupor of dreaming and don't get out of bed. I think about the meaning of the dream, the disabled woman, the stick, the sea, the moon, the pathway.

I tell my grandmother the dream in detail. She says to me, "You're not disabled and you don't lean on a stick. The way is open before you. Just walk." I ask her, as if asking myself, "Walk how?"

But I think I've understood the dream and understood what my grandmother means. What matters is how.

I make myself look beautiful, put on a light summer dress, and go and see Ali at the office.

I sit on his knee and flirt with him. He's surprised by my pleasant mood and caresses me with two laughing eyes. I look into his eyes and try to be a bit serious, but laughter gets the better of me. Ali asks me, "What? What do you want to say?"

I assume the posture of someone about to drop a bombshell. "What do you think about splitting up?"

Of course it didn't explode; the bombshell was defused a long time ago.

"Why? Have you had enough?"

"You know that I never have enough of you."

"Have you gotten jaded?"

"No. It's just that our relationship is messed up."

"That's true."

"And each one of us is trying to end it on their own."

"Then what?"

"So I'm saying what if we agreed to end it together."

"I agree."

"That fast, eh?"

We laugh. Then I tell him I love him, which he knows, and that he loves me, and I know. That a relationship is one thing and love something else. That there isn't a difference or a separation anymore, because he's inside me just as I'm inside him. I'm worried about the love at the hands of this deranged relationship. I also don't want the relationship to end spectacularly.

"Do you agree Ali?"

"Agreed."

"And if I'm weak and call you, you won't answer me. And if you're weak, which I doubt, and called, I wouldn't answer you."

The idea of separation glinting in his eyes, he playfully suggests going to have a beer to toast splitting up.

I hug him, kiss him, and laugh.

"I'm mad about you Ali. Let's have a beer to toast splitting up. But we've agreed, okay?"

I am delighted that we have finally been able to end this relationship in a civilized fashion. I'm delighted to the point of intoxication and I keep congratulating myself on the achievement. I feel freedom, a sense of floating and lightness. Why did Kundera qualify this lightness as unbearable? Lightness is a wonderful thing.

However, once the glow of victory fades, the lightness turns heavy and becomes unbearable. Freedom closes me in and I become imprisoned in a meaningless emptiness. I feel my body, I look at myself in the mirror. I see a person who looks like me, neither a woman nor a man, clear and vague at the same time. The I is there, but not the I known to me.

I don't feel pain and I don't feel joy. I worry that I have died without noticing.

As emptiness grows, my calm grows. I surrender to the numbing of emptiness for an unreckonable time. A familiar longing is born and I do not know how to strangle it.

I stand in front of the mirror and contemplate myself
I am a woman
inhabited by pain
smacked by yearning
I suddenly say in theatrical fashion:
So what, with a shrug of my left shoulder.
I laugh at my overacting
Then
without my volition
longing leads me to the streets
we would cross twice a day at least
I hide among the crush of pedestrians
just my eyes
peeking out from behind the shadows
seeking you and fearful of meeting your gaze
those eyes that strip me completely
of all the mechanisms of self-defense.
In my continual seeking
I often encounter the husband of a friend
whose features resemble my beloved's

when I see him I'm overjoyed
and when I shake hands with him I hear laughter in
    my voice
and see the sparkle in my eyes reflected in his
so I speak to him and look elsewhere
I miss you Ali
and miss myself more.

Days, weeks, or months may have passed, I don't know. No phone calls and no meetings.

Then comes another Kunderian coincidence.

Time: night. Place: Downtown. I'm waiting for a taxi to take me home after a long day amid the books and references in the American University library. His car pulls up in front of me. Ali rolls down the window and asks me what I'm doing in the street at this hour. "Waiting for a cab," I reply, not believing my ears or my eyes.

"Get in."

"What are you doing now?"

"I had work at the Arab League."

Despite the fatigue apparent on his face, his joy at seeing me is unmistakable.

"Have you eaten?"

"Yeah."

"I've had nothing to eat since the morning and I'm starving. Will you have dinner again with me?"

I agree.

During dinner I ask him playfully how the separation is going with him.

"You want the truth, and won't get annoyed?"

I nod my head.

"I didn't notice it."

"Really!"

"I had so much work. Meetings and work visitors like you wouldn't believe. But sometimes I would call you without realizing but, before the call connected, I would remember our agreement and hang up."

He's silent a little, then asks me how I've been.

"At first I was really pleased, then I really missed you."

Then I tell him about my friend's husband who looks like him. He laughs and says that he knows him and adds that all the North Africans befriend each other abroad and fight with each other at home.

We finish dinner and are wrapped in an emotional glow. I ask myself how the evening will end; Ali asks me if I'd like to drink some special wine from his country. My heart pounds, fearful of closeness and fearful of distance. I have the strength for neither.

The car heads home.

Ali brings two glasses and opens the bottle of wine. He tastes it first then pours me a glass.

With the wine I mellow and become more tender, as does he.

He embraces me and whispers sweetly, "I love you."

He floods me with love, warmth, and serenity.

I love this man.

His departure date comes. He says goodbye by phone. I tell him I want to be with him the night before he leaves.

"Don't Ayn. Saying goodbye will be hard."

But I insist.

He's surprised by a pharaonic queen, as he described me.

I go and see him in a long, white, low-cut dress, faience jewelry, and my hair in plaits down my back.

He sees my intention.

"Yes, I'll wed myself to you tonight, one last time."

"Do you still love me?"

"Yes."

"Why?"

"I'd need years to explain."

"Could you summarize?"

I smile.

I remember Rabia al-Adawiya and take a pen and paper out of my handbag and write:

I have known love since I knew your love
and closed my heart to all but you.
I have loved you a two-fold love—
amorous love and a love worthy of you.
In the love that is amorous,
I'm devoted to your praise, you alone.
But in the love that is worthy of you,
you unravel veiled mysteries.

I give him this answer and he reads it slowly. Then he gives me a profound look full of meanings. I see love, gratitude, warmth, melancholy.

I was unable to say anything else after what I saw. I wait until he poses a question. "What does 'veiled mysteries' mean?"

I sigh, then answer. "By you I'm made complete Ali. With you my contradictions are resolved and I'm made whole."

We drink until the early hours of the morning. Then we go to our bed together for the last time. Ali embraces me and comes closer, but my body is closed.

I apologize to him. He closes my mouth with a passionate kiss and whispers in my ear, "Don't apologize."

He wraps his leg around mine, and clasps his hands around my chest.

A few hours later we get up.

He goes into the spare room to pack his bag. I go into the kitchen to make coffee, which I have finally learned how to make.

When we're ready, he kisses me on my forehead. We go out.

He says to me, "Go home to your house from here."

But I insist on going to the airport with him.

He warns me again, "It'll be hard, Ayn."

We hail a taxi. We sit in silence all the way to the airport.

In front of the Departure Lounge he kisses me on the cheek and says, "Keep well."

I grab his arm and don't want to let him go.

"Should I wait for you, Ali?"

"Don't wait, Ayn."

He releases himself from my grip. I follow him with my eyes until he disappears among the throng of passengers.

I am rooted to the spot, like a bride who has learned of the death of her beloved on her wedding night.

2.

I cannot let the last scene pass uncommented; its irony is inescapable. In its melodrama I am reminded of one of the set-piece scenes of Arab cinema, in particular, films of the 1970s and 1980s. There is a pair of sweethearts who have been caught up in a love affair for donkey's years. Our Romeo can't fulfill the material requirements of marriage, and the relationship comes to an end when his Juliet marries a wealthy Arab or big-time businessman. By convention, the young woman returns her engagement ring—if they were engaged—by placing it on the table in front of her ex-fiancé, next to the two glasses of lemonade brought over by a waiter, well rehearsed in this particular scene. The girl exits, and the boy, now over thirty and yet to 'make something of himself,' is left behind. Usually in the next shot we will see the young man sitting in a low-class bar, nursing a bottle of brandy or rum, and trying to forget. He may head for a dope den in one of the neighborhoods of Old Cairo such as Batniya or the Basatin or Imam al-Shafei cemeteries, and join a hash-smoking session. Alternatively, he may go to his usual café, the one where he's been a regular since graduating from university, and where he waits for the letter from the Ministry of Labor appointing him to a state-sector job. For the most part, his friends will advise him to forget the girl, who doesn't deserve him. The young man may get lost in his musings about how to get rich: will it be smuggling or drugs? Next, he imagines himself having become a rich and famous businessman whose ex somehow reappears on the scene. Now he considers getting back together with her, but only after humiliating her first.

What could drive Ali to get married for real to a woman he had never once told Ayn that he loved? Perhaps he just couldn't bear to say something like that to another woman for whom he'd already declared his love. But Ayn had understood that this was a traditional arranged marriage, and somehow she couldn't imagine, in this day and age, even a woman being forced into a marriage with someone she didn't really want, except in the countryside or Upper Egypt perhaps. But he was a man, and middle-aged at that!

It seems to me that the scene is upside-down. From this perspective, and with all due respect to Ayn, I find it funny. But how would Ayn deal with an ending she had known in advance?

She will say to herself
he chose non-love:
I'm a being breathing for love, to love.
There's your place always reserved in the heart
but I must make place for another

others perhaps
thus she decides
when longing grows too much
she'll pick up a book and a mirror
and cross great distances
and from time to time
she'll search in the mirror for two steady eyes
and meet two eyes looking askance
searching for two steady eyes
not finding them
she'll pick up the book and the mirror
and cross distances yet further.

Until she reached Siwa. There, she would let a Bedouin
she has known since he was a prepubescent boy take her to
Cleopatra's pool in the middle of a desert whose moon was
full. She would undress, bit by bit, right in front of him and
enter the water. The Bedouin would strip, all in one go, and
join her. At first she would gasp at the size of his penis, but
in the end she would savage him with the ferocity of a fatally
injured animal. Then she would cry.

Suleiman, the Bedouin, whom she still regarded as a little
boy despite all she had seen of him, took her to a sand dune
at the edge of the oasis. His companions were there meeting
with a group of foreign travelers. The Bedouins skillfully lit
a fire and then cooked dinner. Ayn was delighted to see the
surface of the earth opened to reveal a goat kid cooked to
perfection over a buried wood fire. Despite an abundance of
spoons and knives, everyone, including the foreigners, ate
with their hands. One of the foreigners commented that he
had never eaten goat cooked this way before. "Eat. Eat,"
responded one of the Bedouins. After this rich meal, everyone,

with the exception of Suleiman's companions, grew languid. The Bedouins started warming up tablas and duffas until the skins were taut. Then they began to sing, at first in their language (an unwritten dialect of Tamazight Berber). This was followed by Arabic hymns of praise that made the bodies of the audience sway. A bottle of date arak was passed round. Everyone took a single sip, then handed the bottle on. The arak was very strong and with each sip Ayn entered another world. When they started singing the poetry of Omar ibn al-Farid, she stood up and performed dhikr in the middle of the encircling group. The singer had begun to repeat the same verses over and over:

You possessed my heart, my mind, and my ear
My body, my innards. All of me entirely.
Distance means anguish and closeness mercy
Union is relief when love is my death.

Ayn was sobbing as she reeled among the swaying arms, then she fell to the ground. When she came to, she found Suleiman next to her. Once her eyes had gotten used to the dark she could make out the scattered presence of the others, either in tents or on camp beds. She looked at the now moonless sky with one eye half-open, then went back to sleep.

Everyone rose with the sun. They had breakfast and started to discuss a trip into the Great Sahara. Ayn had believed she wouldn't need to go further than Siwa, but when she woke up with a heavy heart she thought she would extend her stay there. She had never anticipated a journey into the heart of the Great Sahara. Perhaps this would be the remedy for her. She said yes as soon as one of the foreigners suggested she could join them if she wished. She studied the faces and bodies of the group heading for the

Libyan desert, people she still hadn't been properly introduced to. "Not bad," she said to herself. "Not bad at all,"
she chuckled.

She called her grandmother and told her about the trip that
might last for weeks. She also called the woman who looked
after her grandmother in her absence and asked her to sleep
at her grandmother's house until her return. She bought
stuff for the trip and joined the group: three men plus a
woman and her husband, or companion, from Germany,
Switzerland, and Austria; three World War II surplus trucks
and a desert bike belonging to the German guy. Ayn concentrated, initially, on the bike and its owner.

Guided by GPS, the group set off in the morning, heading
north then west toward the Libyan oasis of al-Jaghbub.
Though going was slow and the temperature high, riding the
bike behind Michael was very exciting, particularly going up
and down the dunes when excitement would tip over into
terror. Progress stopped at noon for lunch, then resumed
without break until sunset. While riding the bike, it was
difficult to talk to Michael because of the wind that filled her
ears. Yet in time Ayn grew accustomed to the silence and
concentrated on the whistling of the wind. She clung to
Michael more tightly and said to herself, "The desert night
is long."

Shortly before sundown the vehicles stopped on a sandy
mound close to some acacia-like trees. Everyone got out. The
drivers stretched out on the sand while the others cut up
some dry branches and started to light a fire. Ayn helped to
gather firewood until Michael asked her if she'd like to
explore the area on the bike. Ayn was keen, but did not make
this apparent: she welcomed the idea but pointed out the
need to help the others. Michael replied that there were

enough of them. She got on behind him and they set off for a hill some distance away. They could still see the headlights which had been left on as a guide. Rays of orange sunlight slipped through the low clouds and formed islands, valleys, seas, and mountains. Michael embraced Ayn from behind and used his tongue to nuzzle her ear. "Don't you think it's an amazing sunset?" Before she could think of anything to say back, he had pulled her to his chest and started to strip off her clothes. He leaned her up against a tree and started to kiss her body from the tips of her toes to her ears; Ayn swooned with pleasure and nearly collapsed. Michael raised her thighs with his arms, supporting her back against the trunk of the tree. He forced his way in, he made her quiver and shake until they came in unison, their cries resounding into the void.

The two of them fell asleep. They woke up to the desert chill. Darkness had fallen. After enjoying sex with another stranger, Ayn wanted to examine what she felt. She asked herself what she was feeling. But neither the darkness, nor the cold, nor Michael would allow her to probe her emotions. They put their clothes back on and set off on the bike. Somehow they lost their way. Michael turned a few circles in the direction of what he presumed were the headlights. But he wasn't getting any nearer and even felt the lights were receding. Then the lights disappeared, only to reappear in another spot. The two of them were baffled. The darkness had intensified and the air was chillier. They consulted together and decided to head toward the new source of light. Reaching this was not easy. They went up and down with the dunes, but felt as though they were going round in circles.

They reached the edge of a desolate village whose mud houses were derelict. Nothing hinted at any living presence. They advanced in the same direction until they came close to the source of the light they had seen before. They stopped in front of a house. Almost all of its inhabitants had come outside to investigate the strange noise ripping through the silence of the desert.

"Al-salamu alaykum," Ayn greeted the residents of the house. They responded in kind. Ayn spoke in Arabic and told them that they had gotten lost and did not know how to get back to their friends. "Please come in. Come in," said one of the men of the house whose features they couldn't make out and whose age they couldn't determine in the feeble light emanating from a rickety lamp-post.

The women of the house, whose faces they couldn't see, acted as hosts. Children were entering from all sides. The interior courtyard of the house was suddenly filled with the people of the village. One of the old men asked who they were. Ayn replied that they were a group of travelers and, pointing to Michael, that this was her husband. A torrent of questions began: what did they do, where did they live, whether they had children. Ayn was forced to make things up, which she translated for Michael. This was so he would understand the situation lest someone who understood English or German should appear, talk to him without mediation, and uncover her lies. After a while, to make the tide of questions stop, Ayn feigned tiredness and a desire to sleep. The owners of the house understood, and a woman led them to the guest room. They fumbled their way into the bed, undressed, and started their foreplay. The sound of an engine impinged. It was a vehicle pulling up in front of the courtyard of the house. This was followed by voices speaking German. Their movements quickened. Before they reached their climax, the door opened and a figure announced the arrival of their companions. Michael let out a groan. They got dressed in the dark and emerged to the source of the commotion. Two of their group, having followed the tracks of the bike and the light, had arrived in one of the vehicles. Michael and Ayn thanked the people of the house for their hospitality and generosity and left with their companions.

On the way back, they discovered that they had not been far from the campsite. One of their companions told them that he had fired shots into the air to guide them back to the camp. Michael recalled that he had heard shots but that the wind had taken the sound so he had been unable to work out the direction they came from. After a matter of minutes they reached the rest of the group. Michael recounted what had happened while they ate the cold leftovers of dinner. Some went to sleep in the vehicles, others made their beds on the ground. Michael and Ayn shared a bed for two and resumed what had been interrupted.

What with the very slow passage of time and Michael's incessant chatter about his brilliant motorbike, his riding skills, and the yields of his farm, doubled thanks to the latest technology, boredom began to seep into Ayn. Without wishing to, she found herself comparing him with Ali. But where was Ali now? She tried to imagine him with the other woman. She asked herself whether he let her use his right arm as a pillow, whether he clasped his arms around her chest as he had done with her, whether he breathed her breaths as he had hers. She felt a certain jealousy.

She asked Michael if he had been in love before. He was baffled, as if he'd heard a new turn of speech. He said he only needed a bottle of wine to seduce any woman. Ayn felt revulsion and said nothing.

After the lunch stop, Ayn claimed to be feeling tired from riding the bike. She left Michael to show off his technical skills and joined Georg the Austrian in his vehicle.

Georg initiated the conversation by asking Ayn if she had ever been to Austria. She said no. He told her that he had lived in Cairo for three years in the mid-1970s. "Of course you were a kid then, or maybe not even born," he said with a wink. Ayn matched flattery with flattery, "Of course you came on a school trip to see the Pyramids." He gave a loud laugh and said he had been working for a foreign company in Heliopolis. Then he added that he had always wanted to get to know an Egyptian girl, but that the presence of his wife at the time had prevented him. Ayn smiled and gave him the eye. "Now the chance has arisen from an unexpected quarter." Compos mentis and of his own free will, Georg swallowed the bait and added, "Yeah, the great sand sea splits to reveal a pharaonic beauty." Then he told her he had wanted to get friendly with her from the moment he had seen her at the Bedouin dinner in Siwa, but he had faltered. "After that you chose the motorbike." She commented that she'd never had the chance to ride a desert bike before and added playfully, "Nor have I had the chance to ride a car from the days of World War II." Then she asked him how he had acquired it. He told her about an auction held years ago to sell surplus equipment, that he had bought it really cheaply, that it had been in good shape overall, and that he had changed or repaired some parts and, by the way, he was a mechanic.

One of the vehicles got stuck and the convoy came to a halt. Georg took two metal planks with large cut-out holes from the truck and went to the rescue of the stranded vehicle. Ayn watched the operation from her window and was impressed by Georg's skill and by his strong forearms. She imagined this muscular man in bed. She looked up at the sky. It wouldn't be long until sunset.

The convoy resumed its way. Georg looked at one of the maps and informed Ayn that it wasn't far to al-Jaghbub oasis, but that they likely wouldn't make it that night. Before the sun had completely set, the party stopped near some withered trees and arranged the vehicles in an L-shape as protection from wind and sand.

The men snapped dry branches, and one of them started to light a fire while Ayn and the other woman engaged in conversation. Elisabeth was a nurse from Switzerland and loved traveling. She had met her husband in India when he was studying yoga. They didn't have any children. Ayn commented that the group was well rounded since it contained a mechanic, a nurse, and a farmer. Elisabeth added that there was also Hans, a retired German officer, who loved hunting. Ayn mentally crossed off Hans and, of course, meditating Friedrich, Elisabeth's husband. She had finished with Michael, which only left Georg. She hoped he would live up to her expectations, but she knew looks were deceiving. How many times had she come across a muscled hulk who couldn't keep up with her when it came to the crunch.

As there were practically no fresh vegetables left, Hans took tin cans marked "For NATO Use" out of the trunk of his car. He emptied their contents—fossilized sardines, biscuits, and dried fruits—onto the table reserved for food. Hans started munching, the effect of which was amplified by the prevailing silence. The others glanced at each other and burst out laughing, praising the Lord that the oasis was only a few miles further and that they could endure hunger until the following lunchtime. Hans wasn't bothered by their laughter and continued munching away.

As it grew darker it grew colder, and everyone got ready for bed. Georg asked Ayn where she would sleep. She asked him if she could stay the night in his car, because it was chilly outside. "Of course. And I can warm you up too," he responded with relish.

Her expectations weren't disappointed. In fact, Georg got right into the role of the hunter, as personified by Hans, and ravished her mercilessly. Ayn was in ecstasy and let him devour her as he pleased. When they finished, however, she didn't let him hug her close. She just said thank you. He tried to talk to her, but she pretended that sleep had gotten the better of her and then turned her back on him.

What are you doing, she asked herself.

She didn't answer, but her tears quietly flowed.

In the morning there were only the NATO fossils for breakfast. Hans munched on them and the others decided to wait it out until they reached al-Jaghbub. On the way they encountered a limestone outcrop. The vehicles changed direction to go around. Michael, however, decided to display his skills at jumping or, perhaps more accurately, flying on his motorbike. He fell to the ground from a height of more than sixty feet and ended up with deep gashes on his thigh and a suspected broken leg. Everyone ran over to him. Elisabeth brought the first-aid kit. She bandaged his wounds and made a splint, but the deeps cuts needed surgery. Georg loaded what was left of the motorbike onto his truck, while Friedrich and Elisabeth carried Michael into theirs, where they made him a bed with straps to keep him still when the car jolted.

At the entrance to the town, Ayn asked the first person they met the way to the nearest hospital. The man replied that the town only had one hospital and pointed the way. At the hospital a doctor checked Michael with his hands and stated that it would be best to transfer him to Benghazi General Hospital, which was better equipped. Michael felt nervous and decided it would be best to go back to Germany and have the required operation there. Michael consulted with the group about the ways and means for going back, while Ayn sat a little to one side not joining in the discussion, which was now in German. In spite of her concern for Michael (after a few days in the desert the group had become like a family) she thanked God for guiding her to leave him at the right time, or else she would be laid out on another metal-framed bed next to his.

The final decision was for Georg to take Michael in his car, with Hans following in another, to Tobruk, the site of the closest internal airfield. From there they could arrange Michael's journey to Benghazi and on to Germany, or Italy in the absence of a direct flight. Ayn, Elisabeth, and Friedrich would wait at the oasis until Georg and Hans' return, two or three days later at most.

After the three had departed for Tobruk, Ayn inquired about the nearest restaurant and they headed over. It was a small ordinary place with no menu, and they ordered what there was: vegetables, rice, and camel meat. They ate with appetite, then drank green tea with mint. Ayn asked the person who brought the food about places to visit. He told her about some old tombs and the lake of al-Malfa. In this context he told them about the heroism of al-Sanusi, who was born in al-Jaghbub. Then he asked what their nationalities were. Ayn told him unashamedly, given that none of them were Italian.

The three of them went for a walk around the old town, which was very similar to the old towns in the Egyptian oases with more or less the same mud houses with roofs made of palm trunks. They responded to the greetings of the children who smiled and waved at them. They bought fresh fruit for the day and deferred purchasing other supplies until their companions' return. They would take advantage of their stay in the town and eat in the restaurant. They headed off for the old tombs a couple of miles away. These were very much like some of the Ptolemaic tombs that Ayn had visited in Kom al-Shuafa in Alexandria. They didn't spend long at the tombs and then agreed to go to the desert lake that the man in the restaurant had mentioned. The lake was surrounded by palm trees and somewhat isolated. There were teenage boys bathing and kids playing on the sandy shore. Friedrich moved away from this relatively populous area and went to another spot that, apart from a few wild birds, was completely tranquil.

A body of water in the middle of the desert striped by the reflected rays of the sun coming through the palm fronds: the beauty of the scene filled Elisabeth and her husband with delight. They raced to the lake and splashed each other with water. Then they fused in a kiss and moved further away

Ayn contemplated the wondrous scenery and felt a weight in her heart. She furtively watched the two lovers making love in the water and felt jealous in spite of herself. She didn't envy them, but she was experiencing intense loneliness, profound emptiness, and a sadness exacerbated by having sex without any emotional involvement. Perhaps she should stop doing it. But surely anything was better than nothing at all. She asked herself whether a few minutes of pleasure was worth the spiritual hollowness that came after. The idea made her pause and ask whether everyone felt like her, whether everyone experienced what she called "the spiritual hollowness" when coming down from the pinnacle of pleasure in the absence of love. Surely not, she told herself, struck by the idiocy of the question. Ayn you're petulant just like Ali described you that time.

When it came to petulance, Ayn wouldn't miss an opportunity. For example, she didn't recollect the sweet times she spent with Ali, but invoked the most miserable. She didn't remember him, for example, declaring his love for her in a whisper or imagine him swimming with her right now in the lake. No. But how well she remembered the details of her quarrel with him and his quiet retreat to the other room and her feelings of pain and hurt. She felt angry and flung a pebble into the lake while cursing that man who, she well knew in the depths of her soul, had never stinted in his feelings for her. He just had a fallback position. Because he's not an imbecile like you.

There was no point now in such unhealthy thinking. Ayn came back to reality and decided to do something positive: to have a swim for example or wash her clothes given the abundance of water, and allow herself to resume her internal ranting and raving in the evening once in bed on her own.

The following afternoon, while they were having lunch, Georg and Hans returned. Georg told them that Michael had been extremely fortunate, for when they reached Tobruk airfield the previous evening there had been a plane about to take off for Benghazi. The airport authorities, considering his medical condition, had allowed him to embark and provided him with a stretcher. Hans added that the airport officials had been really helpful in facilitating the other arrangements for him to fly on directly to Germany.

Georg asked Ayn how their time had been, and she told him about the tombs and the lake. They decided to spend the day at the oasis and enjoy swimming, sand surfing, and camel meat.

Ayn was delighted at Georg's return. He was happy too. They spent a really enjoyable time together. But when he started to touch her in the evening, she drew back. He asked her why, but she didn't answer. He persisted, and she replied

84

that she would rather keep her problems to herself. Georg fell silent. Ayn was surprised by her response. It was a phrase of Ali's. Something he would say when she would persist in asking him what was keeping him awake. Had she started talking like him? What did the response mean? She knew that she didn't want to let Georg into her private life, and did want to create some distance so that things shouldn't become too intense. Did Ali think the same way? He would rarely talk about his problems, except if the matter concerned them both. When she would ask him about personal things, he would say it was private. She would get very upset at that answer. Yet here she was giving a similar reply. But there was a difference. Ali and I are involved, were involved, she corrected herself. She had never concealed anything from him, whereas he had concealed his involvement with another woman. In remembering the subject afresh, Ayn felt angry again. She turned to Georg and started to touch him. He yawned and said he wanted to sleep. Ayn swore at him in Arabic and slapped him until he grew aroused. He rolled her onto her back while she laughed. The rest was understood. He didn't let up until she begged that it was enough.

In the early-morning light Ayn discovered the remains of last night: love-bites all over her. She felt ashamed and had to wear a long-sleeved shirt despite the heat.

After breakfast they went to the town market and bought fruit, vegetables, camel meat, spices, green tea, and wild mint. They headed west toward Jalu oasis. At midday they stopped for a light lunch, then resumed their progress. The jolting of the vehicle caused Ayn to hear Michael's motorbike rattling around inside. She smiled as she remembered his love of showing off. She asked Georg what he would do with the bike: he would check later if it could be repaired or reused.

Ayn picked up one of the maps and folded it to use as a fan. Georg asked her why she was so warmly dressed. She showed him the marks he had left on her. He let out a whistle of admiration, then showed her the marks she had left. "I did that?" she cried. "No, it was a wild wolf of the desert," he said laughing. Ayn felt embarrassed twice over, once by his marks and once by hers, but said, "It was a great night." He stopped the car and gave her a long look. She asked him what was up. "You're really weird." She sensed the risk of talking so kept quiet. He started the car and resumed driving. Ayn was aware of what she was doing, and in this light interpreted Ali's silence: a sense of risk; the fear of getting involved.

Ayn decided to teach herself the Indian way of abstinence. She joined Elisabeth and Friedrich in the morning and tried to do yoga exercises. Despite the pain in her knees she made herself concentrate on a patch of sand in front of her or on the rhythm of the wind as Friedrich instructed. In spite of the difficulty in concentrating, especially on the sound of the wind which she found had no rhythm, she still felt that daily practice, especially at this early hour of the morning, was of some kind of benefit to her. Despite the pain in her knees and arms she felt a kind of restfulness, a clarity, a renunciation of men.

She began to sleep on her own in the open air. She watched the stars and waited for one to fall so she could make a wish. But the stars were too quick for her. So she made her wishes even after the stars had fallen. She wished she wasn't separated from Ali.

Even the beauty of the desert with its rolling sand dunes and amazing sculptural rocks could not match the sight of an oasis, its palm trees and pools, glimpsed from afar. At that instant all of them gasped. The silence that the desert imposed was broken. Words and laughter started to flow, and they became playful. The oasis imposed another rhythm. There was eating and gossip with the local restaurant owners, swimming in one of the isolated springs, and dune surfing on the sand surrounding the oasis.

In Jalu, Ayn's caravan was joined by a group coming from the other side of the Sahara. This comprised five Americans who had traveled from Morocco through Algeria to Libya from where they wanted to go on to Chad then Sudan, and in the end reach the source of the Nile.

These Americans preferred to have guides with them. These were drawn from the desert dwellers, and they would accompany them from one region to the next, either continuing with them or handing them over to others. The American group agreed with three guides to take them to the Tibesti Mountains in Chad. These Bedouins joined the group but had their own jeep. They brought with them a kid goat that would be a source of entertainment for the group until the moment it was roasted.

The vehicles moved in convoy with the Bedouins leading the way. Apart from the commotion made by the Americans and their guides at rest stops and the bleating of the goat, which had fallen in love with one of the Yanks, the desert imposed its grandeur on everyone.

After the evening meal, the Bedouins started playing the duffas. Then Abu Bakr, the youngest of the three, improvised songs on various topics, the hottest of which was the goat's infatuation for Robert the American. Robert hated animals as a general rule, and couldn't abide the smell of this goat in particular. But the further away he tried to get, the more the goat's attachment grew. Despite sleeping in the Bedouins' car, the goat communed with Robert all night long. When Robert had had as much as he could take, he demanded that the Bedouin slaughter it on the spot. But they replied that they were saving it for the night of the full moon. The others also objected to Robert's cruelty. One of them joked, "Man, the kid loves you and you want to kill him. Shame on you. You should meet love with love." Everybody laughed and Robert got angry.

Ayn kept up her morning yoga exercises with Elisabeth and Friedrich, and the third woman in the group joined in. She was an American called Gina who worked in journalism and wanted to write a book about the desert.

One morning Ayn was struck by a question. What was she doing in the desert? And for how long? Everyone with her had an aim to their journey: to reach a certain place, to enjoy the experience, to relax, to write. But she, what did she want? She didn't know, but was certain the desert would show her the way. The way to what though?

The night of the full moon was a feast. The vehicles had halted in mid-afternoon and the Bedouins started to light a fire. As the firewood caught light, the goat's communing with Robert took on a more imploring tone. Robert grew more annoyed and walked away from the cries of the goat. He did not return until after it had been dispatched. Even though Robert had been the first person who wanted to devour the goat, at dinner he didn't touch it. One of his friends poked fun at him, "What, are you missing your darling's bleats?" Everyone but Robert laughed. He seemed really torn up about it. The situation prompted another one of Abu Bakr's improvised songs about the goat. This time it was about Robert's belated love for it, and his sorrow and regret over the time he had wasted running away instead of reciprocating the goat's love. The laughter and high spirits continued awhile, then the racket toned down. Ammar, the eldest and head guide, produced a bottle of date arak, which he passed around to the group, who took as much delight in it as they had the roasted goat. Then he asked that everyone tell an entertaining story. Abu Bakr opened with the tale of Robert and the kid, and laughter burst out again. Next Ayn told the story of her grandmother's tortoise which escaped. Two weeks later, it was found a few streets away by the neighbor's son. Some boys were asking a mute child to set a price for it. Elisabeth told the story of the holy cow in India, and how, in veneration, the Indians stopped traffic so that the sacred creature could pass. Georg recounted how Michael's love of showing off to the ladies had gone as far as his launching his motorbike off cliffs, only for him to land with a broken heart and a broken leg. Georg authenticated his words with the pieces of the bike which he still had inside his truck. Friedrich recalled the NATO fossils munched by Hans, whom he asked if he had any left to show the audience. "No. Please no," replied the American woman on behalf of all her group, and she added laughing, "We're familiar with them as we had to live on them for a while." The anecdotes continued until the seventh round of arak.

Then came the stories of passion and desertion.

Ammar stirred the embers and added some wood to the fire so it wouldn't go out. Once silence had fallen over the place, he picked up his flute and gave an affecting musical rendition of the stories that made heads sway. Then he spoke:

> Have the wise of the tribe not said: sacred emotion becomes profane when it ends in union? Have they not also said: the passionate relationship turns to loathing when it ends in consummation? Or is the secret hidden in the nature of love, which dissipates and fades when

it cannot dissipate the object of love, when it does not dissipate lover and beloved together? Is it in its nature to fade if the person does not fade away because of it? Yes. It prefers to die on account of man, if he does not find in himself the courage to die on its account. If we do not sacrifice ourselves, it sacrifices itself for our sakes. As though it insists on renouncing us when it realizes that we are incapable of renouncing it, incapable of offering ourselves as a sacrifice to it, because our selfishness, because our love of life, or what we think is life, makes us cowards in the face of sacrifice, in the face of renunciation, in the face of death. Then caution first awakes in us, and we imagine we can possess love, the essence of love, the visible creation and its hidden shadow, the beautiful woman and the hidden bird of light we have granted this beautiful woman, and we forget love has another aspect; love has two faces: when one is present the other is absent. The two faces of love are two opposite companions, the first is steeped in existence, the second prays for eternity. We reject them both, we reject sacred emotion when we forget the law that states: the one who desires the eternal must forgo existence; when we forget that love will forgo us if we do not renounce it; when we forget that love does not become love, is not called love, if the condition to forgo the substance of love, the object of love, the beloved is not fulfilled. We cannot transcend ourselves and conquer our attachment to a fantasy, that we believe is life, as long as we do not remember that rapture is like God, a proud sovereign unwilling to share existence with another being.[*]

---

[*] Ibrahim al-Koni, *Fitnat al-zu'an* (1995).

Ammar concluded the wisdom of the tribe with another flourish on the flute. Its wailing soared into the sky, reached the moon looking down on them from above, and returned to their ears. Their hearts trembled, and a stifled sobbing ruffled the desert sands.

Ayn meditated on the Bedouin's words that had touched her heart and made her separate from the group and go to a nearby tree to cry privately. Love was conditional on letting go, and she had let go. Hadn't she said to Ali that she preferred being in love to being in a relationship. Hadn't she told him that she was worried about the damage their messed-up relationship would do to their love? He had also let go, but not as a result of the same logic. He wanted to have a traditional marriage, because he wasn't strong enough to love. But he had let you go, let the love object go. He must love you then, don't you understand? So what's the problem? I don't know. Why are you crying? I don't know.

Ayn slept where she was. She dreamed about a woman tied by a rope from the branch of a tree. The rope was tight around the woman's neck, but she was struggling against it. With each pull the woman was upended and swung backward and forward. Her face contorted then relaxed with the swinging motion. Ayn watched the dream with open eyes until the woman's body came to rest. The weight caused the branch to break and the body was released. The thronging crowd gave a cry. There was another woman. Ayn did not know whether to shut her eyes or open them. All she knew was that she did not want to continue this nightmare. She ordered the dream to stop and surfaced trembling.

Cautiously opening her eyes, Ayn found herself beneath the tree she had seen in the dream. Next to her was the broken branch. She screamed and covered her eyes with her hands. Then she ran off crying until she grew tired and came to a halt, out of breath. She lay down on the sand and started to do the breathing exercises she had learned with Friedrich while watching the sunrise until she had controlled her breathing and calmed down.

She returned to the group, most of which had woken up feeling tired and hungover as a result of the arak.

After having lunch at one of the small restaurants in the village, everybody headed to the telephone bureau. This was a small office with only two phone booths and where international calls posed difficulties. Still they waited in line. When Ayn's turn came she requested two calls to Cairo. She checked up on her grandmother and renewed her advice to the woman looking after her. Then she requested a third call. She hesitated. The people queuing pressed her to hurry up. She canceled the third call and left the line only to rejoin it. When her turn came again, she gave the clerk the number. Her heart was pounding as she waited for the call to go through. Then she heard the ringing.

"Hello . . . . Hello."

Ayn tried to answer, but not a sound came out. The clerk came on the line and said, "Please reply, Madam." She heard his voice again, "Hello . . . . Hello . . . ," then the line went dead. The clerk asked her why she hadn't answered. "It doesn't matter, I'll try the number again." Those standing muttered in complaint.

"Hello . . . . "

"How are you Ali?"

"Heyyy. Where are you?"

She didn't want to tell him where she was and asked him if he was doing fine, and he said yes. She repeated the question and heard his laughter. "What? I'm not supposed to be fine?" Anger made her lose it and she exploded, "You've changed."

He denied this and asked her where she was. She hung up and came out of the booth swearing and cursing at him. The clerk stopped her. "The bill, Madam." She paid and walked out looking straight ahead.

Abu Bakr caught up with her. She was crying and told him to leave her on her own. He didn't listen. He told her that it wasn't a good idea to wander around a strange place on her own. Then he asked her what was wrong. She didn't answer. He figured out that it was something to do with a man and teased her, "Don't worry if your husband's gone off with another woman, I'll marry you." She didn't answer him, and he added, "I'll give you one hundred camels as your bride price." Ayn smiled. "Come on then. We're going to go to the lake before we say goodbye to the village."

They rejoined the convoy that was heading for the lake on the edge of the oasis. Gina gave her a novel, *The Alchemist*. "I've read it and don't believe what it says. Just lies and sick fantasy." She handed the book back.

She swam on her own, consumed by anger, hate, sadness. She had no idea what to do. She did not want to go back to Cairo, but equally she could see no point in this journey. She felt an intense desire to fade away. She swam to the far side of the lake, propelled by negativity. She got a surprise while coming back from the far bank.

She looked around, she searched inside, he wasn't there. She dissected her heart, nothing. She was startled. Where had the anger gone, the hate, the sadness? Where had the love gone? Her heart was devoid of feelings. No love. No hate. How could this be? Was it all unreal? She asked herself, "Didn't I love that man?" There was no answer saying yes or saying no. How come? Then she remembered something. She remembered that one day she had said to him she could erase him from her life story and make him as if he'd never been. So, she remembered there was a person called Ali, but the remembrance evoked no feelings. She shook her head in amazement.

Her soul lost, she rejoined the group and asked where she was. They reminded her that she was in the village and that they were getting ready to head south for the Tibesti mountains. Ayn remembered: the Americans would split off and go south to Chad; her group would continue west to Ghat.

At the entrance to a small oasis in the foothills of the Tibesti, the caravan came across gunfire and jubilant young men chanting words they couldn't make out. The members of the caravan joked to each other that they hadn't been feted in this way before. Abu Bakr thought that the oasis was celebrating a wedding and that the group would be lucky to attend the three-day long party of feasting and drumming.

As they went further into the oasis, the words became clear to the Arabic speakers. The three Bedouin and Ayn did not believe what they were hearing, and their faces expressed real bewilderment. Abu Bakr stopped one of the boys and asked him what was up. The boy confirmed what they had heard and the other kids repeated it after him. "America's been hit."

The rest of the group picked up the word America, but didn't understand more. One of the Americans asked what was up. The children chanted, "America's been hit." Abu Bakr translated the news with mixed feelings. However, no one believed him. They went to a café packed with men and boys shouting Allahu Akbar in front of a TV showing the collapse of two burning towers. "America's been hit," repeated young and old. "America at war," announced the screen.

Caught between disbelief, shock, and open and disguised joy, the Americans decided to cut short their trip and return to their country.

The desert has a power cities do not have. What began to assume magnitude in city streets and alleys, the desert brushed off; its winds took and scattered it until not a trace was left.

In Ghat, Ayn and her group visited mountain caves and caverns whose walls and roofs were lined with prehistoric life. Men, women, and animals from the Neolithic wet phase had become visible. Ayn touched them and wished she was among them.

The group decided to continue their journey on to Niger into the depths of Africa. Georg asked Ayn whether she wouldn't like to keep going with them. She didn't know and asked when they would be leaving. The next morning. "I'll think about it and tell you in the morning."

The idea of deepest Africa enticed her, but something was pulling her to keep going west. Perhaps she would reach the ocean she had never seen before. Yet what pulled her was not the sea but the desert. She knew that what awaited her were the cave paintings at Tassili, no different to those at Ghat, and the stone carvings at al-Hoggar. There would be something else. She decided she would go west until this vague something occurred.

In the morning, Ayn exchanged addresses and phone numbers with the group, together with promises of another desert trip the following year. She would miss them, but not keep her promises.

By luck, Ayn got to know another group. A bunch of French enthusiasts for traveling to danger zones, as the organizer of the trip explained. There was no real interaction between her and the French group, particularly the trip organizer, who seemed intolerably vain even to the members of his group. But he had no objections to Ayn joining the group when he learned she was heading west, provided she paid her way.

Pierre, the trip organizer, made use of a Tuareg guide he had dealt with before. Even though Pierre knew the area well, he wanted to add a touch of authenticity to the journey so as to appear more credible to his grumpy group. The Tuareg guide, Tinbuctee, had his head and face veiled with a fifty-foot-long turban. Two eyes the color of ash were all that could be seen of him. He talked little and his voice was low. Nevertheless as time passed, Tinbuctee became Ayn's personal guide. At the Tassili caves he told her that the center of the world was here, that the roots of Egyptian civilization sprang from here, and that when the rains had stopped long ago, the people of the Tassili had migrated east to settled in the Nile Valley. Maybe.

She asked him to reveal his face. He refused.

In between the caves, her previous life, and the desert with its dunes, stone pillars, and rock carvings, Ayn felt she was nearing the end of her journey. She fell asleep in one of the caves. A hunter gave her the Key of Life and a cow. She opened her eyes and smiled. The cow was in front of her on the wall. She called back to mind the image of the hunter and compared it with the carved portrait. "It resembles him," she thought. She sensed it coming back; she sensed it filling her. Smoothly and calmly, like it had left her. Ayn was aware of what was happening to her. Love had come back to her, had come back completely pure, free of all its faults, sublime.

She came out of the cave. Tinbuctee was waiting for her. He read her eyes.

"My journey is finished."

"I know."

On a boulder in the middle of the desert, she sat, the embodiment of waiting, like the posture of Memnon on his stone seat at Luxor's West Bank. From sunset to sunrise she sat, twelve hours of absolute waiting. She did not contemplate the stars, did not think any thoughts, and did not try to find some way to pass the time. She just calmly waited for her appointed moment.

In the morning, she arose from her seat and packed her things. Tinbuctee gave her a lift to Tamanrasset Airport. There he gave her a Tuareg robe as a gift and revealed his face to her. She studied him for a long time. A desert magician. She said goodbye without an embrace.

As an official flicked through her passport at passport control at Houari Boumediene Airport in Algiers, Ayn returned to geographical reality. Baffled and exasperated, the official asked for her entry visa. For the first time, Ayn realized that she had crossed geographical frontiers only marked on maps. She was now in the airport of another state, one that she had entered without a visa. The official asked her again, "Madam, at which border point did you enter the country?" Ayn replied that she had come from the desert, but there had been no borders. The official asked her to be more specific. She answered that she had come from Ghat to Tassili. He looked at her in astonishment, "On your own?" No, she had been with a group. The official took the passport and detained her in a side room. She heard a discussion in a neighboring room: she didn't have an entry visa; she'd arrived from Tamanrasset Airport; she said she came from Libya; Egyptians didn't require visas to enter Libya. Should we give her an entry stamp post-dated? Should we deport her via the embassy? Ayn didn't believe what she was hearing. She had been in the desert, that's what she knew.

The official summoned her to speak to his bosses. The most senior asked the same questions as before. Ayn gave a brief account of her journey from Siwa to Tamanrasset. He turned the pages of her passport and looked at old visas for other countries. "You are aware of the requirement to obtain visas then?" Ayn said yes, but that she hadn't known she would reach Algeria. He asked her about her job. At checkpoints in Sinai, she would usually give a specific response to this question: "Can't you read?" However, under the threat of deportation, she forsook the tone of defiance and acted the model of politeness. With total composure she answered, "Research sociologist for an international organization." He then asked for her arrival date in Algeria. She did not know. How many days had she spent in Algeria. She did not know. The official looked at her in utter amazement. This was a one-off case. In the end the official gave her a retroactively-dated entry visa, and warned her that this would not be repeated. Then he added jokingly that if she were to enter without a visa in future he'd personally put her in prison. She thanked him warmly and promised that it wouldn't happen again.

From the departure lounge she called Ali. To her, his voice came laden with warmth and anxiety. Where was she. In Algeria. What was she doing. Learning patience. When was she coming back. Tonight: "I want you to be the first person I see in Cairo."

In front of the Arrivals hall at Cairo airport, Ali was waiting. A diminutive pharaoh in white Tuareg dress came out. She stopped in front of him and stood motionless with the pride of a princess. Ali looked at her; he was stunned, by her, by the madness embodied in front of him. "You're crazy," was all he could say, and she was in his arms.

3.

Hand in hand, as though we do not want to slip away from each other, our two souls renew their friendship. I am filled with the certainty that we will never part, whatever happens.

On the way, Ali asks me if I've had dinner. I nod my head to say yes.

"Shall we have dinner again, together?"

I look into his eyes and nod once more.

"What? Have you learned patience, or silence?" He makes it a joke since he's not used to sign language, from me in particular.

"What have you got to say?"

His eyes brim with love. But I'm enjoying his burning desire to know my stories.

Then I tell him everything.

He hangs on to my every word and doesn't interrupt the flow. I pause to consider the effect of my absence on him and the impact of my words. He urges me on, "Keep going," while shaking his head in wonder.

"Ali, I didn't do anything I can't tell you about."

"All that, and you didn't do anything!"

We laugh together.

"I asked you Ali if I should wait for you, and you said no," I remind him and myself.

"True. So what couldn't you do?"

"Sleep with somebody you know. Let somebody wrap his leg around mine and link his arms around my chest."

He lets out one of his rare sighs.

"Shall we go?"

"Let's go."

The car is heading for Mohandiseen. I ask Ali to stop.

"Ali, the house is the other way."

"You want to go to your house?" he asks with surprise.

I answer with greater surprise and in disdain, "Well, am I going to spend the night with your wife?"

He pulls up at the side of the road and turns toward me.

"Ayn, I didn't get married."

"What! How come?"

"I didn't get married. Don't you understand Arabic?"

"Ali, I asked you on the phone."

"You asked me if I was fine, and I said yes. That doesn't mean I got married."

I can't believe what I'm hearing. "Okay, but why didn't you say?"

"You didn't ask. You accused me of having changed and hung up."

We arrive at the house. His house. Ours.

Everything is just as I left it the day I took him to the airport to get married. There's no trace of another woman having passed through. I can't find anything to say.

"Some more wine?"

I nod my head. I am confused as to what to do. Despite everything I've told Ali, I find he's genuine with me. He didn't get married. What's this nonsense all about? I remember telling him once that he wouldn't marry her. But what I predicted certainly didn't come true as a result of any supernatural powers of mine. I had lost faith in the principle of one's will resonating with the will of the world. Yet wasn't my purest desire not to split up with Ali? Yes, but I don't believe this.

Ali opens a bottle of vintage wine and tastes it on my behalf. He pours two glasses.

"What are you thinking about?"

"About fate," I answer sarcastically. Then I ask him the question I know he'll never answer at length. We're not in agreement and put off the subject until later as a terse response doesn't satisfy my curiosity. He's never going to elaborate. He changes the subject. Giving me a significant look, he jokingly asks, "The desert magician, that Tuareg man, what did you do with him?" I give a loud laugh and answer in the same jocular tone, "He's the only one I failed with. He never gave me an opportunity." I make a show of feeling aggrieved. "Shame. He got away."

Gently and playfully he pulls me toward him, "And a Carthaginian Berber Arab won't do?"

I draw back, also playfully, "Tsk. He missed his chance."

I feel he is going to pass out from desire for me. I look into his eyes and put the question to myself, "What do you want, Ali?" He misconstrues the question, or perhaps plays the fool, "Don't you want to?"

I find myself becoming more flirtatious despite what I see as the truth of my feelings.

"I've become a Sufi."

"What?" He bursts out laughing and spills the wine onto our clothes.

I love his laughter so much, and the dimples in his cheeks and the gaps between his teeth. God, what am I going to do with this guy.

"Oh man, you've ruined my Tuareg robe."

"Never mind. I'll get you another one." He answers while choking with laughter.

After we've finished the bottle of wine he asks me, "Well, aren't we going to sleep?"

"You bet we'll sleep. Just like brother and sister."

"Like brother and sister. Okay, go to sleep in the spare room."

But the spare room will wait for other times. Its time will most definitely come. As for now . . . .

I let him consume me however he wishes but without any desire on my part. My mind is working faster than the sensory responses of my body. I love you Ali, but I've changed. I've had to sacrifice a part of myself to get to this state of pure love without desire. I feel I'm being dragged into a relationship I've put behind me. Ali knows I'm there with him and also not with him and he stops. "I'm afraid," I whisper as though to myself. "Afraid of what, Ayn?" he says. "I don't know." I start to cry. The tears that got stuck on the day he left flow freely. He enfolds me in a way I cannot describe, full of love, full of warmth, full of esteem. "Please don't cry, please."

In the morning I return home and Ali goes to work on the basis that we'll meet in the evening. I find my grandmother still sitting in her favorite chair just as I left her. I tell her bits about my journey and give her a sand rose as a present. I go into my room to think about what next.

I don't meet Ali in the evening. I call and tell him I'm going to Sinai. He asks me why. I can't find a convincing reason so say, "Because." He doesn't press and wishes me a safe trip.

I know, however, that my fear of spinning back into the relationship is the motive to leave. This fear will also make me learn to dive and have sex underwater. But nothing is of any use. I spend a week in the Sinai, thoroughly cleanse myself in seawater, and come back sea-scented the way Ali loves.

In the office, I tell him everything.

I thought he would be upset, get angry, keep his distance.

But what I say makes him want me more.

Aisha, a mutual friend who has known him well for years, will say to me, "But he'll never marry you after you told him all those things." I will reply that I'm not trying to get married to him. I just love him, and no woman will ever love him like me. "He loves you too. I've seen him looking at you. I've known Ali for a long time, and I've never seen that look before. He'll be tormented by your love Ayn, because he never imagined that he would love so much, and he'll never be able to marry you." I know. I know all too well. I know he loved me in spite of himself. I know he won't marry me. I know that I gave up the substance of love so as to carry on loving.

Am I selfish? The question surprises me. Am I using Ali as a subject for love, as material for a novel, at whose end Ali's role as material comes to an end? Is this procrastination in writing a result of a desire that it should never end? So that the love itself never ends. Am I worried that this love should really end and, for this reason, imprint it as letters on paper? Either to bring it back to mind at leisure in my dotage, or to turn the page and shut the book for good. I'm ashamed of myself, since the question even coming to the surface of consciousness means that some proportion of it, however small, is true.

I put myself in God's hands. I put myself in His hands. Fate will run its course.

I go back to Ali heart and soul. Our relationship becomes better than it was after my doubts and misgivings shrivel up. We spend most of our time together. I finish work and pass by his office. I get depressed reading newspapers and books until he finishes work. We have dinner together then go home. We follow the news: the TV is on all day in the office and all night at home. Together, we will witness the blowing up of mud-brick houses and the flight of women, children and the elderly to the mountains in Afghanistan. We will wake up at dawn one day to the sound of bombs falling on Baghdad. The tears will gel in our eyes in mourning for the civilizations of Mesopotamia. We will await our turn.

I ask him to turn the TV off. I can't bear it any more. He responds that it's his job. Hearing the news makes me anxious and I'm developing an earache. I go to the spare room and lie down on the bed. I try to think happy thoughts. I wait until Ali falls asleep and turn the volume down. I look at his expression. It's calm, as though the news doesn't affect him. He's been through worse, he told me once. I lie down next to him. He senses me, stretches out one arm as my pillow, and wraps the other around my chest. My anxiety fades bit by bit. Here's where I want to be. Forever in these two arms. My whole life long. And after.

I dream that I give birth to his baby girl at the end of the year. A Capricorn like her father. I cradle her in my arms. I'm at a loss for a name. The baby speaks. I'm Warda.

I tell Ali the dream. He listens without saying anything.

"I want to have your baby girl, Ali. I want to tell her about my love for you."

No comment. I see a glisten in his eyes and reluctance in all his features. He breaks his silence, "Don't make things complicated, Ayn." He makes me promise not to do anything behind his back.

I want his baby. But I could never deceive him, like other women do, and confront him with a fait accompli. I don't know which of us is selfish. But I do know that if I did it, against his wishes, I would lose him. I would lose his love and respect forever.

I suppress my longing. But it surfaces from time to time. In moments of serenity I ask him, "Isn't it time to have a baby yet?" One time he laughs, many others he runs away from the question. I get worked up and threaten to get him drunk and take him to the registrar, marry him, and have my wicked way with him. He gets angry and makes a resolution never to drink with me again. He withdraws into the spare room.

I punish him by being distant. But I'm not sure if I'm punishing him or myself. Then I blame myself and remind myself that I am the lover and he the beloved. I am the one seeking, he the one sought. I remind myself of the exalted love that filled my heart in the desert of Tamanresset.

He travels on official business for a week. I await his return with beating heart. I am afraid he won't accept me again. I know I was cruel to him. I beg God's forgiveness for not taking account of His right to Ali and ask Him to release me from the prison of my nature.

I wait for Ali at the airport with anxiety in my eyes. He spots me and his expression becomes happy. I see his delight that I'm waiting to meet him, even though he doesn't like being taken to, or met at, the airport. He embraces me with the familiar affection and love. But his eyes look reproachful and implore me to stop tormenting him. If only I could stop myself from not trusting him, or not trusting myself.

We decide to escape the crush and dust of Cairo, the miserable news, and the political hypocrisy to spend the Eid break together in the Sinai. It's a very long journey, but we make it pass by singing along with bits of Umm Kulthum's "Inta umri." Ali recalls a French girl who cried when she heard the song even though she didn't understand the words. That was in Portugal. Ali talks freely about some of his memories. He laughs when he remembers a night he got drunk in some city with a very beautiful girl and woke up in another city with an unknown and very dumpy woman by his side. I love hearing him talk, even when it's about other women. I urge him to tell more stories and he talks about some of his travels and adventures.

We go swimming in the sea, splash each other with water, make bets with each other over the species of colorful fish, annoy each other, and laugh together like children. We eat, drink, and enjoy ourselves. Life in the Sinai has a different flavor. A mix of Bedouins, Egyptians, and foreigners makes you feel as if you're in another country. But being happy is too much to ask.

In the evening we go to a bar. We sit drinking and talking for hours. Ali comments on some of the Sinai's bad points like the litter and the chaotic building. He makes comparisons between the resort and its equivalent in Morocco. I agree with his opinion, even though I haven't been to the place he means in Morocco. We keep drinking and talk about other things. Then his phone rings. He speaks in his dialect, and I guess the call is from his country. He excuses himself and moves off so I can't hear. Why move off? It must be his fiancée. So they must be in touch. Ali isn't gone long. I ignore it. We resume our conversation, but he senses something has changed in me and asks what's up. Nothing. He orders more beer. It arrives warm. He calmly comments on this.

"If you don't like it, just leave. If you don't like it here, just leave," I snap in irritation.

Ali looks at me unable to believe what he's hearing. He doesn't say anything. We leave the bar and go to a restaurant. He orders fish and more beer. He drinks and ignores the food. I talk to him, but he answers curtly. At the hotel he asks for his papers, which he left with me, and leaves me some money. Uncomprehending, I look at him. "I'm going back to Cairo. Alone."

"Why?" I ask, not understanding the reason for the suppressed anger in his voice.

"You don't know why?"

I become aware of an unmistakable note of pain in his voice. Because of this pain, but without knowing its cause, I start crying. I ask him again, "What's wrong Ali?"

"I'll never let you, or anyone else, talk to me like that ever again."

"Like what?" I ask stunned.

"'Just leave.'"

I repeat the words. "What's the big deal?"

"It's the way you said it."

I don't remember the way I said it. I don't understand the reason for the pain and anger that Ali is feeling. I tell him I don't understand what he's talking about.

"I love Egypt, perhaps more than you do. And I'll never stand for anyone telling me, 'Just leave' here."

"Egypt? What on earth has Egypt got to do with this?"

He packs his bag and gets into bed.

"Ali, I didn't mean it like that. You got the wrong end of the stick. I was jealous. You were talking to your fiancée."

Without turning around he says, "I wasn't talking to my fiancée."

"Ali, I'm sorry."

He faces me, "I'm sorry too."

Then he adds, in a voice that is final, "Please, this is the end. I don't want to see you again."

Apologizing is useless, as is crying. He's made up his mind.

This time
rejection is resolute, final
I've used up many times over madness' permissible
    opportunities
Sorry
he uttered with the finality of a razor
that doesn't allow for debate, appeal, or mumbled
    objection
Sorry
he spat out with the resolve of a dying body
that convulsed during its final moments
to spit out the fever near overwhelming its cells
he spat me beyond the realm of his life
and closed down the openings I used as a trap
to get inside him
he spat me out as the body ejects the parasitic or
    superfluous
or in my case the harmful
Sorry
I froze where I was, broken.

I leave the room and sit on the beach until the sun rises. I feel optimistic as I follow the sunrise and say to myself, "A new day." Ali will forgive me. I go back to the room where he is shaving. "Good morning." He returns the greeting without looking at me. "Ali, today's another day." He finishes shaving and gets dressed. I quickly change my clothes.

"You're not coming with me."

"Ali . . . ."

"Please don't make a scene."

I follow him to the car. I open the door and get in.

"Ayn, please. I don't want you with me."

I stay where I am.

He drops me off at my house after nine uninterrupted hours of crying, and total silence from him.

I call him. He doesn't answer. I send him text messages. He doesn't reply. I write him a letter.

My darling Ali,

I never meant to hurt you. How could I when you're my true love and my soul mate. How, Ali, when you're the light filling my heart and brightening my darkness.

I ask myself why. Perhaps it's a lack of experience, a lack of maturity. Does it count that you're my first love and the first intimate relationship I've given my whole self to, with all my energy and all my naivety. Perhaps that's the mistake, the reason for despair. I don't know. All I know is that I was like a woman possessed, touched if you like. A terrible force, or violence, took control of me, and I couldn't stop it. It's no excuse that I knew I was wrong. I'm not trying to justify my behavior Ali. I'm trying to understand what happened.

My sense of guilt hurts my soul. My mind provides justifications, but my heart does not forgive me. I beg God for forgiveness night and day for having abused His creation, and what a creature you are: God's messenger to me, a gift from the Lord that I didn't know how to treasure.

Writing to you, and perhaps to myself, is my refuge now. You slammed the gates of mercy in my face, but I still hope and pray to God that you'll open them again. Hope is better than despair. May I keep hope for a reunion, if not today then tomorrow, and if not tomorrow then the day after, and if not in this world then in what comes after, when, perhaps, the reunion may be serene.

Your forgiveness, O Lord. Your forgiveness, O Ali.

Yes, there is a difference between being in love and being in a relationship. Love alone is not enough to make a relationship succeed and last. Perhaps I didn't understand you very well, but I don't know how to guess. I'm not the clairvoyant I sometimes claimed to be. How can I know what makes you angry. You would get mad at me because I would quarrel with you at the bar, at home, in the street, in the office. Okay, that's bad. But I found myself asking where should I quarrel with you then. You would answer, well is it inevitable that we quarrel. I would say, it happens that a quarrel is sometimes in order. True these times became more often, but can you have life without fights, anger, blame, without making up? Why not?

Everybody asks me to forget you, and live my life. But you are my life. They don't know how deep my connection with you, with your soul, goes. They all think it's just a relationship like any other. But it's not like that, Ali. And you know it. You're where I live, the place I set out from and where I return, my seventh heaven, my ultimate hope.

O Lord, release me from the prison of my nature.

Can the bond uniting two souls be severed. A physical link may be broken, but the spiritual, Ali, no. O Lord, by *all Your creation, by the whole universe, do not cut me off from Your messenger. I swear to you, O Lord—what do I swear by, I'm scared to swear something I cannot fulfill——I swear I will try and change my nature. Help me, O Lord, and may You forgive me what is beyond me, for You created me this way.*

Was what we had unreal?

Is what I believe in apostasy?

Is my love for you and your love for me a mirage? Even if it were so, I would be satisfied.

Life is very hard despite its many joys, and without love, real or imaginary, it is worth nothing. Life without you Ali does not interest me. Let's start over Ali. There's a promise between us, don't you remember? To meet love with love and loyalty with loyalty.

It brings a smile to my lips when I remember you opening your mouth to receive a piece of chocolate I was brandishing to you. I brought it near your mouth, then pulled it away. You closed your mouth in irritation, piqued and miffed. I held the piece between my teeth and offered half of it to your mouth. You bit it off and bit my lips. You would make the coffee for us, and I would boast to my friends that it was you who made the coffee and, sometimes, breakfast when we were feeling hungry, and my friends were envious of me. We would sit side by side on the couch and sip the coffee. I would steal quick furtive kisses from you. Then, "Come on Ayn, let's go." We'd hug each other. You'd kiss me. Then we'd head out.

You would resent it when, after waking up, I'd keep you in bed next to me. I'll never have enough of you. "Any longing that calms when fulfilled is not to be trusted," says Ibn 'Arabi; I'd say to you "Five minutes more," and you'd ask the reason for these pointless five minutes. That I might wake up with you next to me, my head resting on your right arm, your other arm on my shoulder, your breath against my hair and neck. I miss you Ali. Then, when you made it clear, I stopped keeping you next to me. Now it's a moment when you might fall asleep again or might get up straightaway.

My eleven-year-old child.

Where are the arms you would stretch out and wrap me in while we watched the depressing news on the couch. I'd curl up to you and hide my face in your chest and some-times cry. I know that you don't like to see me crying, but sometimes it happens that I'm too weak and cannot cover it up. Why do we claim to be strong, when we're as weak as we are and need to support each other.

Little boy.

Where has your sly smile gone, the smile that show the gaps between your teeth that I love so much. Where are your fingertips that I never tire of kissing? Where's your lofty nose that takes flight at my teasing? Where are your limpid, compassionate, and weary eyes that soothe me when I kiss them?

I'm waiting. Sometimes I get tired, but I'm waiting.

I usually drink to be able to cry wildly
or to proclaim my opinions with a sometimes
*   crude honesty*
or to enter a state of hysterical staccato laughter
this time
I drink to get merrily depressed
to fill the void with more void
without boredom
or questions

or waiting for something to happen
and not happen.
To your health, Ali.

We did spend happy nights getting drunk together and having a good time. Perhaps you'll only remember me for the nights I got drunk and turned nasty. But there were good times too, when you were happy with me, and I was happy with you.

Love overwhelmed me Ali, but not you. Even if I never love another, it's enough that I knew and lived love with you.

I'm looking at a photograph of you. The one I love but that you don't like. There's suppressed anger in it, and pride; and sadness. Why sadness, Ali? Your anger, honest and open, is preferable to this silent anger. The tightly pursed lips that mean I will say nothing. Your crooked nose, which you don't believe is crooked. Just look at this photo and you'll see. From my perspective bent to the left, from yours to the right. But I like it. I like everything about you except your legs. Two sticks.

When I consider the behavior of other men, I discover I've been ungrateful. None of them match your kindness, your goodness, your nobility, your refinement, or your harshness either.

I believe in the idea that if you really and truly want something, the whole world conspires to bring it about. But at times I worry this is just fantasy fiction. Still there are things I really wanted and hoped to God He would make come true and they did happen, as you know. Does that give me more . . . hope. I was going to write pain. Perhaps they're synonymous, pain and hope. More hope is equal to more pain. Drinking makes me philosophical sometimes.

*But I don't want to get drunk, because when I come round
and find you're not next to me, it's as if the whole weight
of the world has landed on my shoulders. Hope without
pain then.*

> *Breaking the circle is difficult*
> *despairing efforts*
> *like those of cats*
> *in the mazes of psychology research labs at the*
>   *institute of education*
> *I dream of a pregnant woman asking about labor*
> *the pregnancy has come to term*
> *will the circle open and I be reborn?*

Aisha calls me and criticizes my behavior toward Ali.
Then she lets me know the news I've been hoping for with
all my heart. Ali's fiancée has broken it off. I don't believe
my ears, but I'm very happy. She tells me, "Now's your
chance," but that I have to stop fighting with him and wait
patiently for him to call.

But I can't wait. I call repeatedly. He doesn't answer.

O Lord, why do You torture me with my love. Why do I
cry whenever I follow my heart. I imagined hope embodied
before me and I was happy. I know what my problem is. I
refuse to acknowledge reality and prefer to believe my own
fantasies. I only see the signs that conform to my desires and
dismiss any actual indications.

I wake up semi-feverish. I open my eyes and the thoughts
of the night before descend on me. I relive the terror and
pain, and my tears come unwilled. I mourn my situation and
pity myself. I don't know how to escape this trap. I ask myself
why I am crying: I get up and cry, I go to bed and cry. Is it
weakness, fear, loneliness, or despair?

What really makes me sad is that I know you loved me and gave me as much as you could of yourself. But how could you think I intended to hurt you?

I am collapsing.

Excuse me my darling . . . .

I don't care any longer now. Come back or don't come back. I avert my face when I think of you. I reject you inside. Sometimes I do miss you, but I check myself before I submit to my weakness, for you. My weakness corresponds to you. I'm pleased with this new strength. Small pink pills have stopped my tears gushing like a torrential flood, oblivious to the destruction it brings. I took the first pill on top of three beers, and sat observing its effect while it was absorbed. I start thinking, and my mind refuses to think about you. I avert my countenance from you. I feel my attitude toward you is changing. A positive-negative attitude. In the morning I'm convinced I'm better and take another pill. I feel a heavy sadness, and by the middle of the day I find I'm crying again. What has happened. I take another pill. The sadness grows and the pain in my soul intensifies.

I call a friend, a specialist doctor. He recommends another medicine. Different pink pills, triangular shaped. I start taking them and feel an improvement. I feel I am strong, indifferent to things. I will survive. I will miss you. Yes. I will miss talking with you. But I am strong. I don't think much about probabilities. I put the worst in front of me, then imagine new possibilities. Life is full of surprises. I'll be waiting for them. Sadness is no longer a burden. I long to call you, but the self refuses. I don't want to expose myself to pain ever again.

I will go to the Sinai and start over. Restart my life, the one I know and know how to deal with, even if it's

115

not quite what I want any more. I wasn't yours, and I'll never be another's. It's the same for you. You weren't mine and you'll never be anyone's but your own. Is this the pills talking? I'll know when I stop taking them.

Fairouz sings, "My anger with you has lasted so long. I spent years trying to forget you. But I couldn't forget you." I smile at myself, years! There aren't enough years in a lifetime, my love, for us to try to forget.

I wake up the following afternoon with changed feelings. Have the pills stopped working? I'm overflowing with longing for you Ali. I find myself addressing you with the old tones of affection, but they're not old. I miss you Ali, my divine Ali. Am I having a relapse?

My grandmother catches me crying and asks me what the reason is. I tell her what happened. She tells me a comparable story. A few months into her marriage, she was still grumbling about some of the things she hadn't gotten used to and about my grandfather's bullying. On one occasion, my grandfather told her, "If you don't like living here, go back to your own country." She says she was infuriated by what he said and gave him the cold shoulder for days until he apologized and said he hadn't meant it. I say to her that weeks have passed and Ali doesn't answer my calls. She counsels patience until he calms down. Then she goes to her room to sleep. After a short while she calls me and amazes me with one of her outlandish ideas.

"Burn incense for him. Perhaps you've been envied."

In spite of my depression I laugh and shake my head in amazement.

"Nana, I don't believe in the evil eye."

"I'm telling you to burn incense. You've got nothing to lose."

"How can I burn incense for him when he doesn't answer my calls?"

"Go to his office."

"I'm afraid he'd shut the door when he sees me."

"If he loves you, he wouldn't do that."

Carrying the incense burner and a few bottles of beer along with my reluctance and the pink pills (in reserve), I go to see Ali before he finishes work.

He opens the door and is surprised to see me. He doesn't say anything. He leaves the door open and goes into his office. I follow behind him. He sits at the computer and taps away at the keyboard. I sit down quietly and think how to open the conversation.

He starts. He abandons the computer and turns toward me. "Yes?"

I light up at the word while he looks at me blankly.

I gather my courage and take the incense burner out of my bag.

"I've come to burn incense for you."

A sardonic laugh raises the left corner of his mouth.

"You've been envied Ali."

Now he gives a real laugh.

"For what exactly?"

I pluck up my courage, "Me."

"What?" in a mocking tone.

"Your friends envied you for my loving you."

I light the incense and say the incantations while circling round him: I ward off every evil eye that envied without praising the Prophet. I ward off every evil eye that envies you my love.

He leaves me to say the incantations and cense him without passing comment.

"Okay! How about a beer?"

He looks at me from on high, "I won't have a drink with you again."

I take the beer out of my bag and say abjectly, "Okay, drink by yourself. If you had any heart . . . "

He sighs as though he has no strength left, goes to the kitchen, and brings back two glasses.

I secretly thank God, and wait for the beer to have an effect.

I sit by his knees and apologize sincerely. Then I give him the letter I wrote.

He reads it slowly, then puts it in the desk drawer shaking his head with something akin to sorrow.

He softens. "Don't take sedatives Ayn. They're no good."

"I know, but I didn't have any other solution."

"Me too, I haven't been okay."

I say nothing. I've already said enough in the letter.

We go to the Marriott Hotel for dinner. We drink more beer. We watch a floorshow. I notice a woman sitting with a man at the table next to us. Her clothes are overly revealing, as is her makeup, her jewelry, and her crude conversation, part of which I can overhear. I draw Ali's attention to her.

"You want a woman like her."

"Is that what you think of me?"

"Nooo. I'm just joking."

We go home together. On the way I tease him. "I thought you were different. But it's clear you're just like all the rest, a guy who wants a good-looking woman with a smiley face and only as intelligent as he can cope with. A woman who listens, doesn't argue, doesn't complain, preferably a mute. A woman who doesn't get angry, doesn't cry, doesn't laugh for no reason, and who doesn't get ill. In short, a robot."

"Exactly. And thank God you've realized I'm just like other men."

I calm down a bit. I follow the advice of my grandmother not to insist on seeing Ali. I make do with conversations on the phone. I keep my madness at bay until he invites me to dinner. I make myself beautiful and wear a short rose-colored dress and high heels. I pass by the office. He opens the door with affection and a desire to see me again. My nonagenarian grandmother proves right.

We chat away and, before we head down, Ali opens the desk drawer and takes out a large amount of money. He offers it to me.

I ask him in jest, "What's that? An end of service bonus?"

He laughs and says, "Something like that."

Then he looks at me lovingly and says, "I wanted to buy you a present, but didn't know what to get. Please choose something yourself."

I feel embarrassed and ashamed.

Without referring to the subject of his fiancée, I tease him, "But Ali, you'll leave and get married, while I go and have a good time with this money and get involved with someone else."

He gives me the look of someone who knows that I know. He doesn't comment on the subject of his marriage and makes light of the second part, "No problem, enjoy yourself."

"Yes for sure, but I just feel it's not right to get involved with someone else when you're paying. It wouldn't be very ethical."

He laughs while stroking my shoulder.

"Don't let it worry you. Just get another boyfriend."

"It's like that is it? You want to finish with me?"

"Yes . . . ."

We laugh and hug each other. I accept the present and put it in my bag. We head out for dinner holding hands.

I relate the latest developments to my grandmother while kissing her. I see a sparkle in her permanently open eyes, a sparkle of love and of girlish mischief from far-off days. I thank her for her ninety years of wisdom. She reiterates that I be patient in my desire and wait for him to ask for me. So I wait as if dancing on live coals, as the proverb puts it.

Ali calls. In spite of his superior ability to control his emotions, his desire for me slips off his tongue through his words. He invites me to dinner. I tell my grandmother. She laughs and perhaps gives me a wink. "Don't give him a hard time. Try to behave nicely," she says affectionately and firmly at the same time. "Ok, for sure, Nana." Then she mumbles something in Russian. "Are you losing it again?" Laughing, I hug her and go.

I go straight to the restaurant. It's extremely crowded. I look around for Ali and find him at a small table in between a number of others crowded with weekend clientele. I sit down next to him and share his glass until the waiter brings my order. I can see the ardor in Ali's eyes and I become vivacious. He asks me what's behind the change in me. I can't hide anything from Ali. I tell him about my grand-mother's advice. He laughs at length and shows how impressed he is by her intelligence. He asks me if she's tasty. "Ali, she's over ninety-years old."

"So what. She's a woman isn't she?" We both laugh.

With the third beer, my need to go to the bathroom—which I have put off as much as I can so as not to leave Ali even for a few moments—becomes urgent. Nature calls in the end and I excuse myself. The bathroom is busy and there is a queue. I stand in line.

I go back a few minutes later and tell Ali that the bathroom was packed. He gives me a strange look. I'm taken aback, and he asks me dryly, "Did you give him your number?" I look at him questioningly, "Who are you going on about?" He points calmly at a pudgy bald man sitting opposite us at a nearby table who, owing to the crush, seems to be sitting with us. I don't believe what Ali's saying and comment sarcastically, "You think I have my eye on him?" I consider the matter to be over, but Ali keeps going, "You smiled at him." So I respond, "Sure, I smiled at him because he's sitting right in front of me, practically on top of us. Nothing special about that." Then I ask him seriously what's going on. He answers that this person followed me to the bathroom then came back and told his friends that he had talked to me and got my number. I say it's not true, and I look at the guy, who's moved a little away from our table. "It didn't happen." Then I tease Ali, "I didn't think you got jealous."

"I'm not jealous, but I do have my self-respect. If you want to go off with him, be my guest."

I'm stunned by what he's saying and what he's thinking.

"Ali, are you being serious or are you joking?"

"I'm being serious."

"Well I told you it didn't happen. How can you think I could do something like that?"

"What, he's making it up?"

"I don't care about him. I care about how you could have doubts about me. Me, who you know doesn't have eyes for anyone but you. Even if there were a thousand men in front of me."

He says nothing. I look angrily at the man. "God damn him." Then I joke with Ali, "Honestly, you think I'd even dream of talking to him?"

The waiter brings the food. We eat in silence. Ali asks if I'd like some more beer. I ask him what he'd like. He orders two bottles of Stella and the check.

Back home, he changes his clothes in silence. I try to be affectionate and start caressing him. He moves away and motions with his hand for me not to come close. I'm confused what to do, what this is all about.

"What's wrong Ali?"

"You know."

"Ali, you mean the business at the bar?"

"Ayn, I don't like anyone doing things behind my back."

"Ali, I can't believe you're being serious."

I draw near him, and he backs away.

"Ali have you gone crazy? How can you doubt me? Ali, that's an insult."

"I didn't insult you, Ayn."

"No, you have insulted me. And I won't accept this insult."

"That's up to you."

"You're rude and an asshole.

"I'm not rude, and I'm not an asshole."

I leave the house.

Early in the morning I go to his office. He opens the door and greets me curtly. I don't go in. I hand back his gift at the door. He opens his mouth to say something, but I don't give him an opportunity to speak and head down.

I go to the Sinai. I stretch out on a deserted beach and sunbathe. Aisha calls and informs me that I really hurt Ali when I handed back his present. She tells me that his fiancée did the same thing, and that when she tried to get back together with him, he refused, and it was all over. I tell her what happened. She understands my point of view, but reproaches me for swearing at him. I'm also reproaching myself. I've never sworn at Ali before, but he insulted me and has to understand that.

After a few days, I call him. We admonish one another.

I come back to Cairo, to his office, with the smell of the sea, and its salt, on my bronzed body. He greets me with a reproachful look. He opens the desk drawer, takes out the gift, and hands it to me.

"The same amount? No more?"

"You don't deserve more."

We go to have dinner somewhere quiet. Then head home early. The next day he's going back to his country, on annual leave.

Ali departs. I ask myself how long he'll put up with me, and how far.

I don't say goodbye at the airport, or come and meet him. He surprises me a week before the end of his annual leave by returning to Cairo. He doesn't tell me the reason for cutting short his vacation, and I don't press. He resumes his job in Cairo, and I spend the week with him at home.

He goes out in the morning after we drink coffee together. He calls me from the office at the end of the day and asks me if I need him to get anything. I spend the day tidying the house. I download different recipes from the internet and learn to cook because of Ali. He seems impressed with the food and thanks me. Then he jokes, "But tomorrow we're ordering out." I laugh and ask him, "You mean the food's no good." He's quick to deny this, "No, no, I didn't mean that. But there's no need for you to exhaust yourself." At home Ali sees me in all my states: covered in dust, with matted hair, tired out and, in the end, beautiful.

A very belated scene, I say to myself. I should have lived at home with Ali for long periods right from the beginning.

Although I treat the house as my own, I haven't been able, after several years, to find a spot I can call my own. Despite there being three bedrooms and three living rooms, I search every corner for a place that is mine. All I can find is the couch Ali and I sit on. I miss the disorder of my own room in my own place, my books, my personal things, a small worn doll from my childhood. I love the house because Ali lives in it, but it's not his house either. That's over there, back home in his own country.

Sometimes we go out for dinner with friends. Then we come home and drink wine. One such evening, after we had finished a bottle of wine and mellowed, I stretch out in Ali's arms and ask him, "Ali, you won't ever leave me will you?" He answers me with an intense love and in a voice whose beauty I don't know how to describe, "I'll never ever say no to you. You don't know how much you've fulfilled my life."

"Really, Ali?"

"What, you don't know for sure? You don't know that you've taken possession of me?"

"Okay. And if you get married?"

He doesn't answer the question but says something more beautiful than any conceivable answer to a hypothetical question.

"Perhaps this temporary relationship is more real than any marriage."

"Okay then, why get married?"

"I didn't say I would get married, and if I did, it doesn't mean I'll fall in love again."

"Ali, I'm ready to leave behind everything here and come and live with you."

"That's tricky Ayn. Tricky."

He hugs me closer to his chest and wraps his arms round me. We sleep on the sofa, fused together.

We don't meet for weeks. Preparatory meetings, the Arab Summit—and we're at rock bottom: emergency summits, as though we were surprised by events we help to create. With all these emergencies, unforeseen guests land up at Ali's house. Ongoing political nonsense. We continue over the phone, but I'm not satisfied. I want to see him, touch him, inhale him. He apologizes.

At difficult times, major crises
when it's beyond us to do anything
except mourn
perhaps our being together becomes a positive act
my being with him reassures me
his being with me doesn't mean much
crises are greater than us
and our being together
from his perspective
becomes an extra burden.
Difficult times and major crises grow day by day.
What's in my hands to do?
I began hoping to meet him and imagining rejection
to lessen my desire and forestall my dejection
despite every self-defense mechanism
when he rejects my desire
none of these precautions are of use
and a new bout of depression hits.

Ali invites me out to dinner. He is accompanied by Mr. Basheer, his friend and boss, and Aisha. During dinner, Aisha and Mr. Basheer have an argument which ends with Aisha, who seldom cries, in tears. A prickly love affair nurtured by bitterness. Ali tries to calm Aisha down, but she gets up from the table and leaves the restaurant. A tense atmosphere normally makes me panicky, particularly if it's to do with feelings. Despite my desire to stay with Ali, I think it might be best for me to go too and leave him with his friend. However, Ali asks me to stay, and we all leave together for his house. I'm surprised. Ali never takes me home when he has guests. I'm overjoyed.

Back at the house we knock back more whiskey. I wait for it to have a positive effect then tell Ali's friend off for making Aisha cry. The effect is negative. He gets angry and curses all of us in a way I find laughable despite my astonishment. Ali laughs too. Mr. Basheer leaves the room and comes back with another bottle. I put on a tape of classical music to calm the atmosphere down. Leaving Mr. Basheer to his own business and his drink, I sit on Ali's knee and flirt with him. I chastise him for his absence and he apologizes, blaming the requirements of his job and the circumstances. I threaten him in a playful tone with leaving him and seeing someone else. He responds calmly, and with what seems to me indifference, that I'm free. In a second, or less, I jump up from his leg and curse him and love and the relationship. Mr. Basheer makes a noise. I become aware of his presence. I look at Ali. I realize the disgrace I've caused. Ali will never forgive me. "Ali, I'm s . . . ." The word sorry does not come out of my mouth. It's become a meaningless word. Mr. Basheer leaves us to it and goes to his room. I spy anger and regret in Ali's eyes, but he doesn't utter a word. He pulls the cover over him and closes his eyes. I stand in suspense for a few minutes, not knowing what to do. Then my legs carry me to the spare room.

After weeks apart, he didn't express any unexpected enthusiasm when I suggested spending the following evening with him.

"You'll be sleeping in the spare room."

I hate meetings with preconditions.

I kept quiet.

"I'm being up front," he said.

"Not entirely."

"No, I'm being totally up front."

Silence.

Conversation curtailed with the promise of a date.
A date not definite.
My fear grows. The meeting will be nerve-wracking.
I go over things with myself.
I imagine different reactions all ending up the same way
tears, a fight, estrangement
endless anxiety.
I spend the whole night trying to picture one bright
  possibility.
My confidence wavers at what I see. Perhaps he's right.
Perhaps it's best for us not to meet again.
He's going back to his country, to his life in which I
  have no part
and never will. That's what he's decided.
But my heart tells me that the decision isn't final.
I'm only certain of one thing
that he's the man I will fall in love with every time
  we meet
and he advises me not to meet him
I discover that I love loving him.
I'm scared to meet and consider apologizing.
Maybe he'll ask why when I insisted
maybe he'll breathe a sigh of relief and praise my
  assessment of the situation
maybe he'll apologize for his being too busy
and I'll thank him for the effort, of uncertain result,
  I don't have to make.
I don't like my hesitation.
I decide to go on the date and let events take their course.
But I don't like to be weighed down by all these
  "maybes"
I want to see him so I can love and pamper him and
  be pampered by him

I want us to sing together "Raqq al-habib"
I want to wrap myself in a short shawl and dance
    for him
the famous dance of Carmen, for him alone.
My heart is heavy and misgivings condense
I drink a cup of coffee in the morning
I turn the cup around and consider the signs.
Indecipherable.
I call him. He answers with an indecipherable voice.
Things shrivel inside me
"If you come, we'll drink coffee and you'll go home
    to your place."
I'm silent.
He waits for my answer.
I cry off the date.

Then we meet.
We sit long hours in the same place
we drink beer and exhale smoke
we look in every direction except ours
I see him without seeing him
he sees me without seeing me
we sit face to face without connecting
I'm in despair at my hope
I ask him if we'll split up
he neither denies nor affirms
I interrogate his eyes
impenetrable
I ask for pen and paper from the waiter and write:
"Better for this heart to throb"
I pass it to him
he reads it slowly then carefully folds it
and tucks it in his shirt pocket.

We resume silence.

Aisha invites us to celebrate her birthday. I go from my house; Ali comes from his. At the party we meet several mutual friends and others I don't know. Among the various women at the party, there is one in particular, from the same country as Ali, that I'm put off by. Her thinness is excessive, her movements robotic; her steps are measured, her laughter florid. She is armed with the full armory of feminine pursuit, and is in a state of calculated readiness, waiting to pounce on her victim. She is like a colorful mannequin in a shop window, dolled up by the shopkeeper without style, but she has a price. I glance at her trying to dance.

Despite the general good cheer pervading the scene, my chest feels tight. A vague sensation that something is going on around me, behind my back, takes hold of me. I shut myself off in the personal space of my dancing. I dance feverishly, and without stopping, to a rhythm only I can hear. I am drunk, hungry, ravenous, and exhausted. Ali asks me to stop dancing. I don't stop. Everybody goes to the buffet, while I remain in my feverish circle. He brings me a plate of various kinds of delicious food. I shake my head and look into his eyes, "There's something not right, Ali. Something not right's happening."

"Ayn, you're drunk. Have something to eat."

I refuse to eat and continue dancing until the morning, until that woman leaves the party and the place is empty except for Ali and Aisha, who goes to sleep in her room. Ali tries to get close to me. I draw away staggering, but I don't fall over.

He asks me what's happened to me
rapture happened to me.
I didn't love you, I was enraptured by you

and you don't know what rapture is
love is demanding and not satisfied.
How to reach the object of my love
when there is no reaching
just attempt after attempt
union without attainment.
Rapture is the way to unify with the desired
with God, with the higher self
Who has reached God? No one.
You are my higher self
who reaches you, who tries to attain you.
Me,
I am your lover that strives
but does not want to reach
since attainment ends desire
you are my end on the path
the way must be arduous
or else why make the effort
but God does not flee desire
God does not flee the desired
God spoke to Moses and showed the way to Mohammed
led him to the Seventh Heaven.

I wake up at Ali's house. His arm is resting on my stomach.

I don't feel guilt, or pain, or fear of losing him. I feel a deep calmness welling up from inside. I think about myself. His anger, his rage, his decision not to see me again no longer concern me. I'm what concerns me. I feel a calmness I haven't felt before. I don't need him anymore. My own self is enough.

I turn toward him as he sleeps. He's not my man any longer. He's become a strange person to me. I carefully remove his arm and stand up.

I leave.

4.

B y the light of a small torch Ayn read Henri Charrière's *Papillon* the whole way to South Sinai. This was human behavior laid starkly bare under the microscope of prison. Crime was latent in the human soul, concluded Ayn after finishing the book, which she had loved despite the horrific nature of some of the scenes. In some way she understood the world of criminality, and even found it more gratifying and alluring then the world of values, praiseworthy morality, and fake refinement. She dozed off contemplating the behavior of society's outlaws. She dreamed of the birth of the new moon and smiled through her dream. At dawn she awoke from the dream at the entrance to Dahab. She was greeted by the sea breeze laden with the scent of iodine that she loved. She looked at the sky and did not believe her eyes. She had just dreamed about it. The new crescent moon.

She blew it a kiss on the sea breeze. She was optimistic about new beginnings. She expected life's surprises.

She went to the Desert Moon camp, right on the sea, and registered. She put her stuff in the hut and changed her clothes. She thought that the sea would still be warm. She swam eastward until she came face to face with the sun, which was slowly coming up from behind the mountains that loomed over the sea on the other shore. She welcomed the sun and prayed to it in her special way.

She returned to her hut and lay down on the mattress on the ground. She invoked the moment of the new moon that she had seen in her dream and embraced it until she fell asleep.

She woke up in the afternoon hungry. She ordered lunch from one of the workers at the camp and sat on the beach. A small boat was approaching from the sea and anchored in front of her. Two people jumped out: one was a Bedouin and the other a foreign man with very long wavy brown hair. He was breathtakingly handsome. Ayn was rooted to the spot. This young man came up to her with a big fish, "Would you like fish?" She responded as though in a trance, "No thanks."

The guy vanished and didn't reappear until Ayn had finished eating. Without asking permission, he lighted on her table like a starving hawk. "Do you want the leftovers?" She shook her head. For an instant she thought he worked at the camp and would clear the table, but he sat down and greedily finished off what was left on the plates. "Thank you," he said and left. Astonished, Ayn observed him as he moved off. She asked the camp's manager, "Who's that?" He replied with a laugh, "That's Apollo, from Corsica." Then added, "He's a bit weird, but he's decent and harmless." She asked him whether he lived at the camp, and the manager nodded his head and said, "But he doesn't have a hut, he sleeps on the beach." Ayn's curiosity grew and she asked him, "And what does this Corsican do?" The manager shrugged his shoulders and said that he didn't know of a specific job, but that he sometimes fixed the plumbing in the bathrooms in exchange for food and a place to sleep.

In the evening she went to a nearby pub with some girl-friends. She spotted the Corsican near the bar and pretended to ignore him. She sat down with her friends at a table close by him and observed him discreetly. He was also deliberately ignoring her, but his eyes were on her table. After a little while, she went up to the bar and spoke to the barman, whom she knew. Before going back to her table, the Corsican stopped her. "Can I ask for a favor?" Shrugging her shoulders, she told him he could. "Tell the tall girl sitting with you that I'm the man she's been looking for since the day she was born." Ayn looked at him and said to herself that this man was insane. Nevertheless she relayed the message to her friend. "Tell him he's the ugliest man I've ever seen and makes me want to throw up." Ayn went back over to the Corsican who asked what her friend had said. She said she was involved with someone, Ayn smiled at him. She invited him to have a beer, but he said no and left the bar. Ayn rejoined her friends and they discussed this strange guy. She told them what he had done when she had lunch. They told her that they sometimes saw him herding goats and picking up the dates that had fallen off the palms along the beach. Nobody really knew anything about him. Ayn said dreamily that he was very good-looking. The friends laughed as they construed a glint of adventure in Ayn's eyes. They asked her what the plan was. Ayn answered intently that she wasn't sure yet; he was a new type for her. She would have to think carefully before making a move. But she was happy that her friend wasn't in the least interested in him, because Ayn didn't like getting into competition with a friend for the sake of a man. Men were pigs and didn't deserve to be fought over. That had been the friends' opinion for years. But Ayn would say to them that Ali was different, he was a decent man. They would laugh at her, "Let's see how long your opinion of him lasts." In spite of everything, Ayn still esteemed and respected Ali.

Ayn went back to the camp after her night out. At the entrance to the camp, she stumbled over the Corsican wrapped up in a makeshift bed. He woke up with a shock.

"Don't you look where you're going?"

"Does anyone sleep in the entrance in the dark? You're crazy." An argument began in the middle of the night and only came to an end with the intervention of the camp manager, who asked the Corsican to go and sleep on the beach, or rent a hut. The Corsican gathered up his old bed and shuffled off to the beach muttering in his Corsican dialect that nobody understood, although the swear words, which the ear can make out in any language, were clear enough.

Ayn went into her hut and locked it. She slept with a very broad smile on her lips. The adventure had begun.

Before sunset on the following day, the Corsican with his long wavy hair reappeared. Ayn was watching the sunset and waiting for Apollo to start a conversation. Her instinct hadn't failed her. He came up to her on the beach and asked her to kindly accept his invitation to dinner. Ayn gave a sarcastic laugh, "How are you going to invite me when you beg food from the patrons?" He gave her a sharp look, "That's not your concern." She declined his invitation with an air of superiority. He left, came back at the same time the next day, and repeated his invitation. Ayn declined. On the third day, she accepted on the condition that she paid her share. He didn't object. She asked him at what time, and he said now. She considered his appearance, "Are you going in those shorts and plastic flip-flops?" He looked at himself and saw nothing strange in his appearance. "Why not? Besides I don't have anything else." A social scientist going out with a bum!

They went to a restaurant on the beach. Everybody welcomed him warmly, "Hey Corsican, how are you?" Ayn ordered fish, he ordered chicken. "I like to catch fish, but not to eat it," he said. Ayn didn't ask for any explanation and ignored his comment. They ate in silence. Then Ayn paid her check, and the Corsican thanked the restaurant owner for his hospitality. Ayn was about to burst with curiosity, but she was training herself to control her behavior. On the way to the bar where they had met three nights before, the Corsican said how impressed he was with her independence, and Ayn expressed her amazement at his insouciance. He pretended to get angry and shouted, "Do you think I eat and drink for nothing. Of course not. I work and provide services." Ayn asked him to lower his voice. They reached the bar and ordered two beers. Then he explained his malady to her, "I think I've been mentally ill for two years. I can't hold money in my hands or carry it in my pocket. I can't deal with money. That's why I do odd jobs and get paid in the form of food, drink, and somewhere to sleep. A friend of mine puts the rest of my earnings in the dried belly of a shark." Ayn listened in wonder, and tried to hide this from Apollo's piercing eyes.

He suddenly asked her about her work, and she replied that she was a part-time social researcher, that is, she undertook fieldwork when asked to do so by some institution or organization. He asked her what research she was currently working on, and she replied that she didn't have a project presently, although she had been thinking about the criminal underworld At this, the Corsican let out a whoop of delight and opened his arms wide. "I can't believe my luck. I had a feeling I'd find someone to study my case." Ayn looked at him quizzically. "I'm going to tell you something I haven't told anyone here. I feel I can trust you."

He began to recount his, and his family's, history of criminality. This continued until the morning.

Ayn held her breath as she listened to stories of drug dealing, prostitution, and murder, of grandparents, sons, and grandchildren who had lived their lives in prison or been born there. She asked herself what she was doing with this delinquent. He went to the bathroom, and she breathed a massive sigh of relief. She considered leaving quickly before he came back, but something kept her seated in place. She knew, rationally, that this person might be dangerous. Not might be, for certain, she told herself. She knew, intuitively, that she was attracted to him like iron-filings to a magnet. She decided to make a run for it, but didn't move. The Corsican came back to the table with two beers.

Apollo asked for her sociological interpretation of his narrative. Ayn said that at first she had thought he was making up stories, some of whose mythical sheen went beyond imagination. But she had reconsidered on the grounds that no one would boast of such a quantity and variety of criminality. She remained silent for a little than added in a low voice as if talking to herself, "It's genetic, a virus in the family."

Suddenly, she kissed him on the mouth.

He was surprised, but appeared grateful. She had kissed him and not been put off by his past. She had kissed him as he was. She hadn't judged him or put him on trial.

It was dawn when he asked her where she'd like to watch the sunrise. She pointed to the Qabr al-Bint area by the sea. They walked a few kilometers along the beach, and on the way she tucked his arm under hers. He leapt from her side as if he'd been stung by a scorpion. "Don't hold me by the arm like that. It reminds me of prison." She apologized. She hadn't meant anything. She hesitated before asking him what prison was like. He told her lightheartedly that the first three years had been enjoyable because the prison was full of his friends, rich Columbian drug dealers. There had been hashish, alcohol, guitar playing, and dancing. The following seven years had been seven lean years. The friends had been dispersed to various prisons. He had tried to escape several times unsuccessfully and his sentence had been increased.

They reached the remote diving spot. They undressed and swam in the sea under the light of the large crescent moon that was vacating the sky to a sun preparing to rise. Then they lay down on the sand and looked up at the sky. He gently turned her onto her stomach, then raised her up a little to assume a position of prostration. Ayn let him move her and adjust her position as he wished. He inserted his penis into her ass, by degrees, and with a skill that meant she felt no pain. Then he began to squirm around inside her, he rammed, relaxed, rammed. Ayn felt an extraordinary pleasure that she had not experienced before. But then he touched a certain spot inside her and began to increase his pressure. She let out a moan of pain in a voice that, to her, seemed another person's. Ayn tried to ignore this spot and concentrate solely on the pleasure. He gently increased his pressure and expansion deep inside her, and made contact with that spot again and again. She shouted at him, "Stop!," but he continued and, again, she ordered him to stop. He kept up his thrusting so she pushed him away with what was, to her, unnatural force. "What happened? Did I hurt you?" he asked when he saw that she was trying to hold back her cries and that her eyes gazed in shock or, perhaps, horror.

When she had looked at him she had seen the demon inside herself in his eyes. He had seen the horror in her eyes. She had realized intuitively that this man could kill her. She hadn't answered his question, and he hadn't pressed. They walked silently until they reached the camp. Ayn went into her hut and locked it without saying a word to the Corsican, who stood puzzled, not knowing what to do at this early hour of the morning.

She placed the pillow over her mouth and gently released another portion of her pain. This Corsican had gone beyond the circle of her pain and crossed her boundaries. A historical pain she had inherited from previous lives, a pain she lived on and that lived on her. She didn't know its source exactly, but she did know it cleaved to her soul. She also knew that it was connected with Ali. Throughout her relationship with Ali she had never felt this pain. It was as if he had medicated it for her without her having being aware of its existence. Perhaps she had surrendered her soul willingly and never been afraid. But this Corsican, some day, would pluck her soul, if she didn't watch out for herself. She wanted to call Ali. She wanted to take refuge in him. But she didn't know what she would say to him. She didn't know how he would react to her call. She called his number and hung up before the call connected and he'd see her number.

Ayn cried. She was scared of herself because she knew she was scared of the Corsican and desired him. She would never be strong enough to get away every time she gathered up her things to escape.

Apollo vanished for a week. Ayn occupied herself getting to know the customs of the Sinai Bedouin and trying to write a research proposal. But her mind was scattered, and her eyes were roving, on the lookout for the Corsican. Ayn wished he would disappear for good. But in the depths of herself she was waiting for him to appear out of nowhere and provoke a storm of excitement and wonder.

She sat on the beach with a book by her side. She spied Apollo's hair streaming out at sea. She felt something drop in the pit of her stomach and, in spite of herself, she held back, picked up the book, and pretended to read. He anchored the boat in front of her and shouted in his exhibitionist way, "Come on, I'll take you to a beautiful place I found yesterday." He spoke to her as if resuming a conversation that had been interrupted five minutes previously. She claimed to be busy. "You're lying, you've been waiting for me for a week. Come on." How had he known? He was sensing her desire and her confusion. "Come on, it's a full moon tonight. Don't waste time." She got up from her place. He sprang into the boat and stretched out his hand to her. She climbed aboard. She found a large mirror, a backpack, and some tins. She asked Apollo about the mirror. "You'll find out later on." The boat sped off despite the head wind. Ayn returned to high spirits as she was sprayed by the waves. She stood at the front of the boat and spread her arms to meet the waves. Apollo stood behind her and also opened his arms, declaring, "Titanic." Ayn gave a loud laugh then said, "I don't want to drown at sea for the fish to devour me." The Corsican kissed her. "Don't be scared, you won't be alone, we'll be together." That was precisely what made her scared: their being together.

They reached a rocky beach with a derelict house that Ayn had heard talk of before. A few palm trees provided some shade on a patch of stony ground. Apollo asked her if she had seen the house before. She shook her head. The house was haunted by the ghosts of its masters. Nobody, not even the government, could buy or sell it, or knock it down or rebuild it. No one knew the whole history of the house, but many repeated the tales of those who had tried to stake ownership to it. "Do you see the stone wall that's fallen down?" Apollo pointed to the eastern wall. Ayn looked in the direction of the wall. "The man who tried to break the stones was struck with paralysis. The man who wanted to live in the house without the consent of the masters' ghosts was afflicted with various illnesses, whose only explanation was the ghosts' anger." Ayn felt excited and nervous. She asked Apollo why he had brought her to this desolate place. "I slept here last night, and the ghost of the house's master came to me and asked me to find the lost key. When I do, the house will be mine." Amazing! Yet the doorways to the house were open, what was the need for a key? Whoever found the key would become the house's master with the blessing of the ghosts, and nobody would trouble him. The Corsican explained all this to her while they were wandering around the stone house that overlooked the sea.

Ayn stretched out in her bathing suit on the shady patch and imagined herself, dripping with sweat, searching intently for the key until she found it a few feet underground. This place would become hers. The Corsican brought the mirror, his bag, and the tins from the boat. Then he splashed her with sea water to rouse her from her fantasies, the content of which he had discerned. "The house is mine, not yours." She answered from the middle of the room overlooking the sea, which she had decided would be her bedroom, "The house belongs to whoever finds the key." He pulled a small bottle of Egyptian whiskey out of the pocket of his bag. He took a gulp and handed Ayn the bottle. He lay down next to her.

She waited for him to touch her, but he didn't. She stroked him with her fingertips, and he flung her hand roughly aside. Ayn got annoyed. "Is this what you want?

Foreplay followed by sex followed by orgasm? I gave you something better." Ayn sighed in the knowledge that he was right. He had taken her further than ordinary orgasm. He had taken her to pain and released that part she allowed him to. She knew that he gave of himself, and that she granted him the pleasure of freeing her from the pain. But in truth, she did not grant him anything. He took that from her himself. But, yet, he couldn't take if she didn't allow him. She was in control, and not him. She was the one who let him enter as a man and let him come out a child.

He asked her in a domineering tone to strip and assume the prostrate position.

She let him infiltrate into the interior of her soul, and released a larger part of the accumulated pain. Then, when he tried to take complete possession of her, she screamed with all the force of self-defense against a mortal threat and pushed him away from her. "I'll never hand over my soul to you, never!" She let her tears fall copiously and freely.

He drank some more whiskey, then moved away until she calmed down. Ayn looked for a paper and pen in his bag. She wanted to write down what was happening to her. She tried to read her feelings and emotions. But she didn't know where to begin: from the pain that predated her existence or from the unconditional happiness she had lost when she extracted herself from Ali's arms. Was this the same pain Adam and Eve felt when they were expelled from Paradise. Have all of us inherited this soul-piercing pain, or has it condensed just in my soul. And who was this Corsican? She put the paper to one side. She took a few swigs of whiskey and got ready for the moon to rise.

It rose slowly, bashfully, bearing Ali's face. She didn't believe her eyes. It was him, with his eyes, his crooked nose, and his tightly pursed lips. He was observing her anxiously but without anger. She looked at him with a vague accusation and wrote:

Like the moon
that does not wait for someone to await its arrival
like the moon
that does not announce its appearance or prepare
    for it.
Stealthily, if you're not attentive, it slowly rises
without spectacle or introduction
from behind the blush mountains on the opposite
    seashore
a reddish orange disc
laying a reddish orange path cutting the darkness
flirting with my toes at the edge
inviting me without invitation to cross
I throw myself on the path bewitched
it rises and I swim
halfway along it withdraws its light
my breaths are cut short and I flounder
like the moon he's a darkling star
only illuminating by reflecting sunlight
he reflects her light in his turn
but in essence he's dark.
In Arabic the sun is feminine and the moon masculine.

The morning sun caressed each of them separately, and they awoke accordingly. They bathed in the sea, then had breakfast from the tins that Apollo had brought. The Corsican began his chattering. Ayn ignored him. She still wasn't completely awake and didn't like conversation in the morning. Apollo lit some dry wood and made tea.

He brought the mirror and propped it against the trunk of a palm tree. Ayn watched him as he opened his backpack and took out a plastic bag. The Corsican looked at her and asked if she was ready. She gave him a questioning look, "Ready for what?" He answered her in earnest, "To be made whole." She poked fun at him, "Do I look as though I'm missing a limb?" He ignored her sarcasm, opened the bag, and took out what was inside. Ayn gasped, "What's that?"

He stripped her of her clothes and positioned her in front of the mirror. "Shut your eyes." He tied the object he had taken out the bag around her waist and secured it with two clips. "Take a look at yourself now." She opened her eyes and looked. At first glance she was shocked as she stared wide-eyed at her reflection. Then she laughed. She gave the plastic dildo, erect between her legs, a shake. She was impressed with the way she looked and rubbed the big male member attached to her woman's vagina. "Now you are Agadistis." She turned to him while still holding her erect member and asked him, "Who's Agadistis?" He told her about the daughter of the sky-god Zeus by the Earth Mother who was born with both male and female sexual organs. How the gods were frightened by Agadistis' twofold power and castrated her. Ayn groaned loudly with resentment at these stupid gods who had deprived her of this other organ. She skipped around in front of the mirror and watched the movement of her penis bouncing in front of her, and her laughter rose. The Corsican stood next to her, and the two of them rubbed their penises in front of the mirror, making each other laugh.

"Now it's your turn." She gave him a blankly questioning look. He adopted the position of prostration and asked her to penetrate his ass. Ayn blanched. "Come on, I'll guide you." She shook her head in confusion and didn't know how to respond. He turned round to her. "What's up with you? Don't you have a penis now? Use it!"

"Apollo, are you . . . ?"

"No. But I only possess this orifice. I'm not a woman. And you're not a man. Come on."

He resumed his prostration and guided her how to insert the plastic dildo without injuring him. Ayn swallowed her saliva with difficulty as she watched what she was doing. Then she gradually began to accommodate herself to her new role and listened to Apollo's moans. She saw herself; she saw her subjugation in this position.

His moans increased with her pressure. She could also feel pleasure, and something else. She was exercising her power over him, controlling his pleasure. She suddenly withdrew her penis then thrust it up him once, and he screamed in pleasure. She did this a few times until he screamed at her to stop and he made her come out of him. "Don't do it with a man's way of thinking. Be the way you are, a woman."

She tried again. She penetrated him delicately, she exerted gentle pressure as she forced a way inside him, and she felt with her penis the barrier of his ass. Then she pressed gently and opened a passage for her penis inside him. She felt as though she had entered a tunnel. She felt Apollo's breaths which he was trying to subdue. She forced her penis inside the passage until he screamed. A different scream. A scream that resembled hers. "Enough, enough, I beg you." She stopped. He rolled onto his back in exhaustion. He looked at her with teary eyes. She saw what he had seen the dawn he had touched her pain.

"No woman before you has reached what you reached."

Ayn was also exhausted. It was as though she had donned another soul from a past life. She removed her penis.

She washed it in the sea and put it back in the plastic bag.

"Marry me. We'll make the world a better place," said Apollo.

"We'll give birth to a monster who'll destroy the world. Don't you see we're alike. Don't you see the demon possessing us."

"We are the new gods. Believe me."

"I want to go back to the camp." She went to the boat.

They returned to the camp. He invited her for lunch. She declined the invitation.

"I want to be by myself. All my energy's been used up. Go away now."

Her words didn't please him, and he threatened her that if she repeated them he would vanish forever.

"That's up to you."

She went inside her hut dazed, tired, and dejected. She threw herself on the mattress on the ground. She fixed her gaze in space until she fell asleep with her eyes open.

She woke up before sunset. She prepared a cup of coffee. She spent a while searching for two eyes closer to slits, but did not find them. She rinsed the cup and made another coffee. Extra sweet, medium, just a hint of sugar, without sugar. She turned the cup in different ways. She looked for a hint of him. Then she noticed it in the midst of many familiar and unfamiliar faces. Her soul took comfort. She could make out the words 'ud, come back, eid, feast, and 'ahd, promise. Yet that night she dreamed about him having gotten married to a woman whose features she couldn't clearly discern. She woke up at dawn and recollected the dream. There had been a simple family celebration. Ali had seemed calm as usual, smiling. Ayn hadn't felt angry or even surprised. She said matter-of-factly, as though she were speaking about someone else, "Ali's going to get married."

Without thinking she called his number. He answered her warmly.

"You're still up at this hour?" she asked with surprise and affection, not as if they hadn't spoken for two months.

"I'm leaving in a few hours."

Ayn noted that this was the time of his summer vacation.

"Ali, you're going to get married."

He laughed, asking her how she had known. "I dreamed about your wedding."

Ali was silent. She could almost read the astonishment on his face.

"Who is she?"

"I'll tell you later, after the wedding is over."

"I know who she is."

"Who . . . ?" he asked with a kind of flirtatiousness, and incredulous that she could know.

"I don't know her name, but I saw her at that party at Aisha's."

He neither confirmed nor denied.

"What's your news, Ayn?" he asked with genuine concern.

She told him everything all in one go. She heard the shock through his silence.

"Ali . . ."

"What are you doing with yourself, Ayn?" his voice came choked with emotion.

"But you're the one Ali who . . ."

"You're the one who left, Ayn."

"My heart sensed that something was going on behind my back. And guess what, you're getting married," she said vehemently.

"Ayn, get out of that place right now and come back to Cairo."

"I'm scared Ali, but I can't come back. I'm drawn to him."

"That man's dangerous. He might hurt you even if he doesn't intend to."

He fell silent and waited for her to say something.

"Ali, I wrote a poem about you. Can I read it to you?"

"Go ahead."

She read him what she had written while waiting for the moon to rise.

"Beautiful."

"Ali . . ."

"Yes . . ." he replied in a voice that had become tender and mellow like before.

She said the words she had wanted to say from the beginning of the conversation.

"I really miss you."

"Me too Ayn, I miss you."

"Would you have left without saying goodbye?" she chided him softly.

"I knew you would call."

"Okay, try to sleep a little, and call me when you get back."

"Ayn, take care of yourself. And drop that guy."

"I'll take care of myself, okay. Hang up then."

"You hang up first."

"Okay, I'll count one, two, three, and we'll hang up together."

She counted one, two, three, and listened.

At almost the same time, the two of them said, "Why haven't you hung up?"

They laughed together, and Ayn felt a gush of joy. Joy like the joy she had lost so long ago that she no longer reckoned its passing in ordinary years.

"Okay, I'll hang up. Keep well." He hung up.

Ayn kissed the phone. She had missed the warmth of his voice, his calmness, his sweetness so much. The crazy

Corsican had drained her. She went back to bed in a state of delight. Happy because she had gotten back her friend, the one she could tell everything. Happy because she had felt Ali's love for her, and that he was worried for her.

She awoke at noon and wasn't certain whether her conversation with Ali had occurred in a dream or for real. She checked the call register on her phone. She *had* called him at dawn. It had happened then. The phone rang and she answered, without looking at the caller ID, in the voice of someone still awakening from a dream. It was Aisha, who told her she had taken Ali to the airport and that he was going to get married. "I know," Ayn replied calmly. She added that she had called him a few hours earlier. Aisha asked her if he had told her who the bride was. "He evaded giving an answer and said he would tell me when it was over. But I know who she is." With burning curiosity Aisha asked, "Who?" Ayn reminded her of the party she had had, then described the woman in question. "Salma!" she exclaimed in amazement. "She's a friend of Ali's ex-fiancée. That's impossible."

"He'll marry her Aisha, you'll see," Ayn said with total conviction.

"I thought he'd marry Karima, the other woman who came with Salma."

"I kept my eye on both of them. Karima wants to have fun with Ali, spend a night or two with him. But that Salma was acting like woman stalking a husband," Ayn replied while she reconsidered some details of the party. She felt a delayed anger building up inside. She ended the call and went to the sea.

She swam. She reviewed her conversation with Ali and felt elated. She remembered the woman whom Ali would marry and became angry. Between elation and anger, she turned round toward the beach looking for the Corsican. She didn't find him.

Why the anger, she asked herself. Was it because she still loved him or because he was getting married? Because he had arranged his wedding during their relationship. Again. She went over his remoteness during the past few months, his quietness when they met, his insistence on sleeping alone. And the party, the vague signs. She cried in spite of herself and cursed him privately. She hated him for getting married to her opposite in every respect. Perhaps if she had been better than her, or even her equal, she wouldn't have gotten so angry. But he had chosen someone beneath her in every way. She wished evil upon him. She decided to exact her revenge. She would hurt him like he had hurt her. She would give him a big plastic penis as a present and recommend he use it with his wife. She knew how Ali would feel then. She knew what a traditional eastern man he was. She knew the magnitude of the offense. Perhaps that would be the last time they would meet. Let it be. There was no longer anything worth regretting.

The phone rang. She looked at the number. Unknown. She picked up, and heard the voice of the last person she'd have thought of. She didn't believe her ears and gave a delighted cry, "Geooorg!" She had totally forgotten this character and the whole Great Sahara journey. Immediately, she invited him to spend a few days with her in Dahab. He agreed and asked about the bus times. There was a bus at midnight and, as it was direct to Dahab, this was the best time. "Till the morning then," he said.

"I'll be waiting for you at the bus station." Ayn hung up shaking her head in incredulity. She recalled the time she had spent with Georg and smiled. Fate has its ways. He'd come at the right time.

She was surprised, next morning, by Apollo outside her hut. He asked her where she was going, and she told him she was going to spend a few days with an old friend. He claimed to be jealous and said in his histrionic style, "How can you go out with someone else? I don't like to see my girl with another man."

"Relax, we'll go to another camp." Then, as if she had suddenly become aware of what he had said, she added contemptuously, "Who says I'm your girl?"

"Me. Aren't I your man, and you my girl?" he answered in a humorous way and kneeled down in front of her. "Didn't I ask for your hand in marriage?" Ayn ignored his performance and said seriously, "We're not in a relationship, Apollo. Make sure you understand that." Then she headed for the bus station.

Ayn welcomed Georg with genuine affection. They went to a Bedouin camp on the other side of Dahab. They relived some memories of the desert journey. She asked him about Michael. He told her that he'd had an operation on his leg, but still had a slight limp. They spent the day in the sea. After that, Ayn intentionally made them go to places that Apollo frequented. She finally spotted him at the disco. She pulled Georg's arm and stepped onto the dance floor. She pretended she hadn't seen him, but she spied real jealousy in his eyes. She waited for him to come and say something to her, but he left the place.

With the surprise appearance of Georg, and in the absence of acrimonious feelings or unique sexual experiences, Ayn, to some extent, restored her psychological balance. Being in several relationships, Ayn concentrated solely on herself: she didn't think about any of the three men. In some fashion she reverted to her childhood. She played about in the sand, digging moats and building castles. She would feel sad when the waves washed the castles away and flooded the moats, then she would laugh and start again. But when she had sex with Georg, she discovered that she had lost something. She had lost her old sense of pleasure. She was shocked by her desire for the ebbing and flowing pleasure around the circle of her pain.

After three days, Georg said goodbye to Ayn and left her to her shocking discovery. Ayn went back to her camp, packed her bag, and decided to return to Cairo. Aisha called and told her that it really was Salma whom Ali had married. "Let him enjoy her," Ayn responded indifferently. She cancelled her trip and went to the bar. She drank until inebriated. When she saw the Corsican, she went over to him and said through her tears, "I accept."

He took her far away. Without taking her clothes off he penetrated her. He let her leave him inside her until she had assuaged some of the pain, then he pulled out. They went back to the camp. Apollo went to sleep on the beach, and Ayn went into her hut and slept deeply until morning.

She awoke to the bleating of goats. When she came out of the hut she found Apollo waiting for her in a pickup truck with seven goats in the back. He urged her to hurry up. She looked him over with sleepy eyes. "Come on, we're going to Cairo. I'm going to ask for your hand from your grand-mother." Her eyes widened in amazement, and she opened her mouth to say something. She suddenly remembered that'd she said she accepted. But she hadn't thought he'd take the matter seriously. She looked at the goats tied up behind the cabin of the vehicle, and asked about them. He answered with enthusiasm that he'd inquired about the Egyptians' customs regarding marriage and learned that he had to offer an engagement present and a dowry for her. Ayn still didn't understand the reason for the goats' presence. She asked him, while shaking her head in wonder, "Where's the present and dowry?" He pointed at the goats. "You'll marry me for seven goats, Apollo! Have you lost it?" and she laughed. Apollo explained to her that this was the advance, with the rest to come in twice-yearly installments, according to the goats' own cycle of pregnancy and birth. She liked the idea. Apollo asked her if her grandmother would agree to the marriage. "I'm sure my grandmother will fall in love with you, she's also got a touch of madness about her." She quickly took a shower and changed her clothes, then she contemplated Apollo's appearance and said, "But you can't meet my grandmother in those shorts and plastic flip-flops."

"You're right!" He instantly disappeared and came back ten minutes later wearing the jeans, shirt, and shoes he'd had on when he came to Egypt. "I only wear them on important occasions," he said as they took off for Cairo.

On the way he asked what her grandmother's name was. Ayn was puzzled, for in fact she didn't know. Everybody called her Nana, and the letters that arrived from Russia bore her married name, Mrs. Rabia al-Saqi. "I think she's called Natasha," Ayn replied in a whisper.

They arrived at the house. Apollo carried four of the goats, and Ayn carried the other three while imagining her grandmother's reaction. She opened the door and called out, "Nana!" The grandmother was surprised by the goats running around the living room. She looked at the calendar on the wall and said in amazement, "Is it eid?" Ayn burst out laughing as she hugged her grandmother. "They're my dowry, Nana." The grandmother became aware of Apollo's presence. "Who's this?"

Ayn replied while she was still laughing, "The groom." Apollo cleared his throat, gave the grandmother a bow, and kissed her hand. She smiled at him, and he took encouragement. "Madam Natasha, please allow me . . ." The grandmother interrupted him, the smile having vanished from her lips, and said, "My name is Veroneshka." Apollo gave Ayn a furious glance and shrugged his shoulders. "I didn't know."

Apollo recommenced his performance. He gave her a bow, kissed her hand, and said with gravitas, "Madam Veroneshka, please allow me to ask for Ayn's hand in marriage." The grandmother regarded him in silence. He explained to her the theory of goat husbandry, stressing that in a few years she would have wealth, in goats, to the tune of half a million pounds. Ayn followed this incredible conversation while suppressing her burning desire to laugh. Apollo fell silent and waited for an answer from the grandmother, whose face had remained expressionless. She shooed away the goats and pointed to the door, "Outside!" Ayn burst out laughing, and Apollo opened his arms theatrically and begged, "Naaana." She pointed to the door, "Outside!" then turned to Ayn. "As for you, if you insist on marrying him," she said, pointing to Apollo, "you'll lose your inheritance." Ayn repeated the word "inheritance" as she fell about laughing. "Nana, do you call the bric-a-brac you brought from Russia an inheritance?" The grandmother swatted them all away like cholera-bearing flies and shut the door.

Apollo accused Ayn of being the reason for the grandmother's refusal. Ayn shrugged her shoulders. The performance was over. "If I hadn't gotten her name wrong right at the start, she would have agreed. I know what women are like." They put the goats back on the truck and went back from whence they'd come.

Some days later, Apollo hired diving gear for him and Ayn from one of the diving centers he dealt with. He asked Ayn to accompany him to a remote diving spot. Ayn asked him why he had chosen this out of the way location. He told her that he hadn't chosen it of his own accord: he had slept in the haunted house where the master's ghost had come to him and asked him to search for the key there. "Really! Okay, what if *I* find the key?" Ayn asked in a tone of defiance. "You'll give me the key. You wouldn't deprive me of my own house, would you?" Ayn sighed as she said, "Hmm, I'm not sure. Don't rely on my generosity."

They prepared the tanks, put on the suits, and entered the sea. Ayn tried to explore underwater at some distance from Apollo, but he didn't leave her on her own. He had told her more than once that she was the only person he could trust, but when it came to the key he couldn't rely on her. They stayed at a depth of thirty feet, delving among the rocks and coral reefs until the gauges on the air tanks showed that the oxygen was almost used up. They came gradually up to the surface, feeling exhausted. As soon as he was floating on the surface, Apollo shouted in anger, "That's impossible. The ghost told me that this was the place, at thirty feet."

They rested a little. Apollo closed his eyes and traced with his fingers, as though he were reviewing details on a map. He leapt to his feet and swapped the empty tanks for full ones. They made another, fruitless, attempt.

At the third attempt, they each spotted the key, which was jammed between branches of coral, at more or less the same time. Apollo's hand, however, moved more quickly than Ayn's. He grabbed firmly hold of the key and pulled it out from among the branches. He cut his hand in the process, and the key slipped from his grasp. He grabbed Ayn's arm and tried to pull her away, but with her other hand she managed to snatch hold of the rusty key. He kept a grip on her arm until they surfaced.

"Give me the key," he panted.

"No," she insisted, also panting.

He let go of her arm. They took off the diving suits and put the gear in the car.

The whole way back, Apollo tried to persuade Ayn to relinquish the key. She refused with exceptional stubbornness. She didn't in fact know why she was holding onto it. The house didn't interest her in the slightest. She didn't believe in the whole thing and thought Apollo's stories were bullshit. All the same she hung onto the key. "You'll regret it, Ayn," Apollo warned her with a terrifying calmness. "There's nothing for me to regret, believe me," she replied without looking at him. They reached the camp. Ayn got out of the car and said with childlike delight while waving the key, "See you later." Apollo answered in a voice whose strangeness she didn't note the time, "See you in Hell."

Ayn hung the key round her neck and lowered it under her blouse and onto her chest. The following day, she stopped a taxi and asked the driver to take her to the house. The man shouted in fright, "The haunted house?" and refused point blank. She stopped another car and the driver agreed to take her to the closest point to the house. She would walk the rest of the way.

She opened a bottle of beer and put on a Frank Sinatra tape, "My Way," in celebration of her sanctioned presence in the haunted house. Then she went back and forth all over the house looking for the keyhole to fit the key. But she didn't find it. The key was bigger than all the keyholes. After all that effort! She had doubts that maybe this wasn't the key the ghosts had talked about. "It doesn't matter now. I'm in the house." She lay down on the beach and exposed her body to the afternoon sun until it set, leaving in its wake that deep pink color that slowly turned a sorrow-inducing indigo. She remembered Ali: talking to him face to face; the way his laughter grew expansive when he teased her like a child; the corner of his lips that he sometimes twisted to the left in mockery of her opinions; tickling the end of his nose, a discovery that no one had made before her, and his astonishment at her, and perhaps his own, discovery of this ticklish spot; the 'no' in his eyes; the feel of his skin on her skin; his smell like that of a newborn baby. I miss you Ali. I miss myself.

She went back into the house and illuminated all the rooms with candles. She played the Frank Sinatra song again. "My Way" echoed through the whole house, went out of the missing windows to the sea, and returned to her lying on her bed in the room which she had previously decided upon as her bedroom.

She awoke in the morning to her screams. Her grandmother, her parents, whose faces she only remembered from the wedding photo that hung on the wall in her room, and all her friends, all of them were deformed, afflicted with leprosy and paralysis, drinking alcohol, and laughing horrifically amid ruin and fire. Apollo was in a child's stroller, smiling at her with the smile of a child who had lost innocence.

Ayn shivered despite the heat that she could almost feel burning her skin. She put her hands to her face and cried.

She had just seen him, like he had said, in Hell.

Ayn went to the camp unable to shake off the image of Hell. She found Apollo in front of her hut. She pulled the key off her neck and gave it to him without a word.

She went into her hut, packed her bag, went to the bus station, and returned to Cairo.

As soon as she heard he had returned to Cairo, Ayn sent Ali a short text message. In spite of her anger that he hadn't gotten in touch with her even though he'd been back a week, she chided him gently, just writing, "I expected better." As if Ali had been waiting for this sign, he called straight back. Just upon hearing her voice, he called her by a dirty word he had learned from her. This word would, from this conversation on, become the sole verbal expression of his absolute love for Ayn. They made each other laugh while interrupting each other. It was as though each of them had missed speaking to the other for ages.

"How's your marriage?" teased Ayn.

"Shit," replied Ali laughing, even though his response bore the confusion of a man who had just lost his freedom.

"Never mind, you'll get used to it soon." Ayn heard schadenfreude masked in her voice which Ali picked up on, "You're gloating!"

"Honestly . . . yes," she said and laughed loudly. She asked him if he was at the office and he said yes.

"I'll come by."

She put on a pale pink dress that emphasized the suntan she'd acquired in the Sinai, and went to see him.

She examined him like a mother whose only son had insisted on going to the front in a war that didn't concern him, and had thrown himself into unnecessary danger. She stepped back and came close. She felt every part of his body as though she were making sure he was still whole, that the frog-lady hadn't eaten any part of him. He trembled at the touch of her hands, and laughed, "What?" She shook her head saying, "Your hair's gone grayer," and added playfully, "So much for a happy ending, Ali." He laughed as he extracted his body from her hands. "Do you think it's all over for me!" Ayn stuck her tongue out and her look said, "Your ending's with me."

Though he had crossed the middle ground, and seemed as if he had made up his mind to marry that woman and gone there, his voice and his eyes hinted that his decision wasn't final, that he hadn't completely crossed the border, that he was still swaying in that thorny region between here and there.

She sat on his knee and kissed his eyes. All of a sudden she jumped up and sat in the chair opposite. Ali read her puzzlement and stretched his arm out to her and sat her on his knee again.

"Your status has changed Ali. I don't know anymore what's allowed and what's not."

He asked her about Apollo. She related developments and told him about the image of Hell he'd sent her in her dream. "I saw all my friends except you Ali. You escaped Hell." She continued talking as though to herself, "Perhaps being married to another woman is better for you."

"Are you jealous Ayn?"

Ayn thought for a little, then answered no. He expressed surprise. She asked him frivolously, "Are you jealous of Apollo?" He didn't answer, and Ayn explained for him, "I created my space inside you by my efforts and by the way you were with me in joy and pain. You also created your space inside me by your personality and the way I was with you, in all the moments and different emotions we lived through. Salma can't take my place, she can create her own place inside you according to her efforts and actions. Apollo can't take your place, but he has created his own space inside me in his own way."

Ali hugged her tight and kissed her forehead. "You mean you're not angry Ayn?"

Ayn fell silent for a while and seemed to hesitate. Ali urged her to speak, "Say what you're thinking Ayn."

"I'll tell you, Ali, because I can't hide anything from you."

Then she confessed.

"At first I was really angry, not because you got married, but because you arranged it all behind my back and because you married my complete opposite in every way. I felt betrayed."

She looked deeply into his eyes and said in a tone laden with despair, "You know what I wanted to give you as a present?"

Ali shook his head in sorrow.

"I wanted to give you a plastic penis."

Ali was stunned. He opened his mouth for a few seconds then closed it again and put his hand to it. Ayn continued her confession.

"I wanted to hurt you Ali. I wanted to take revenge. I wanted to wound you like you wounded me."

Ali forcefully exhaled the air he'd been holding in. He was looking into her eyes to confirm what she was confessing, however he knew she didn't lie. "Did you really want to do that?" he asked her in a voice strained by emotion.

Ayn nodded, "But my heart didn't obey me. Over time the anger went away, and the love remained."

Ali was silent for a while, and Ayn too.

"I'm sorry Ayn."

Ayn hugged him tight and kissed him all over his face.

"A mother can be angry with her son, can hit him, kick him out of the house, but she can never abandon or reject him."

"True."

She saw gratitude in his eyes.

"Okay, aren't we going to have a beer."

"We'll have a beer."

Spontaneously, Ayn went to Ali's office and spent the day with him. He let her sit on his knee and kiss his eyes howsoever she wished. But he moved his lips away from hers the moment he felt himself surrendering to her.

Ayn insisted they go to a bar near the office before Ali went back home to his wife. She snatched another hour with him. They drank several beers in record time. Then she finally had to let him go. Though he felt he was returning to prison, he didn't state it explicitly.

Once Ayn had prepared herself mentally to accept his wife in their life, she told Ali that she was ready to love Salma and treat her like a sister.

"Are you sure, Ayn?"

"I'll try, Ali."

She asked him to invite her to dinner at his house. He promised he would once he thought the time was right.

Ayn was surprised by a phone call from Apollo. He told her to save his number. She asked him where he'd got a mobile from. "Extra effort, believe me." Ayn sensed there was a woman involved. He confirmed her intuition, since he couldn't keep anything from her. "You must come to Dahab. You have a rival."

Ayn answered without fuss, "I'm the last person to get into a competition over you, Apollo. You're well aware of that."

"I know, but come. I'm having a birthday party. I'll be thirty-three. That was the age when Jesus was crucified."

She said she would think about it, but made no promises.

She went to see Ali and told him about the conversation with Apollo. "Are you still with that criminal?" he asked disapprovingly while shaking his head in amazement at her affairs. "There's something that draws me to him Ali," whispered Ayn in a troubled tone.

"Ayn you're free to have relationships. But take care, I beg you. I won't say this to you again. That man is suicidal, he might hurt you without meaning to."

Ayn gave a deep sigh and told Ali, "That man touched my pain, Ali. I need him." Ali shook his head in denial of what she was saying. Ayn added, "I need him so I'm not pushed back toward you. I need him because to some extent he makes me balanced, or perhaps he represents the crazy aspect of me. I don't know. But I'll go mad Ali if I carry on like this."

Ali listened to her in silence.

"I'm going to Dahab tonight."

"Take care of yourself," he said to her, his eyes pleading with her not to go.

"When I come back, I want to have dinner with the two of you at home. I want to eat meat," she reminded him jokingly.

"*If* you come back," he said doubtfully.

"Of course I'll be back. I can't endure Apollo's company for more than two days."

She gave him a farewell kiss on the eyes and headed for the bus station.

Ayn called Apollo before she got on the bus to Dahab. "I'll be waiting for you at the bus station. I've got a surprise for you," he said excitedly. Ayn replied with coolness, "You're full of surprises Apollo."

She mixed coca cola with some whiskey Ali had given her for the road and quickly took large gulps so she could sleep.

She reached Dahab after midnight and found Apollo waiting for her inside a luxurious black Hyundai car. Apollo got out of the car and opened his arms in his usual way. "Darling! What do you think?" he said, pointing to the car. "Don't call me 'darling' again. Get it!" Then she walked round the car shaking her head. "It's clear she's a very rich woman," commented Ayn. "And very old," added Apollo laughing. "She reminds me of my grandmother. Come on."

They took off in the car toward the haunted house. Ayn remembered the vision of Hell, and she told Apollo she didn't want to go there. Apollo gave her a knowing look and reminded her, "You're the one who insisted on not giving me the key, and scoffed, 'See you later.' Where would I see you then, except in Hell?"

Terror built up inside Ayn, and she took refuge in silence and gripped her small bag tightly.

Apollo kept talking and recalled an event from the past. "You know, when I was in prison, the social worker refused to let me direct a play I'd written, and she brought in a director from outside. She was pregnant. I said to her that she lived in freedom on the outside while I was a prisoner in a wretched cell. I warned her that if she insisted on keeping me from directing the play, I would poison her breast-milk, and her baby would die."

Ayn turned to him horrified and asked what had happened.

"She insisted on depriving me of my right. So I poisoned her milk, and her baby died."

"Apollo, I don't want to go to that house," she said remembering Ali's warning to her.

"Ayn, don't be afraid. I'll never hurt you," he said with a note of truth.

She knew he loved her, but she couldn't trust him.

Apollo did a U-turn and headed back to the bars and restaurants. "Let's drink some beer until you calm down."

At the haunted house, Apollo told her about Melissa: a businesswoman worth billions who would be up in arms if her millions in commission were one dollar short. But Apollo always hoped she would lose a few dollars, because on those occasions she would penetrate him with all the anger and hatred in the world. She would almost tear his ass to shreds, but his pleasure increased in proportion to her losses. Ayn didn't know why he was telling her these details. Was it random or did he intend to arouse her.

"But she's stupid, she thinks she can buy me with her money."

Ayn gave him a dubious look.

"Why are you looking at me that way? Do you think I'm after her money?" He gave a loud laugh. "Do you know what my bank balance is from my past drug dealing?"

Ayn shrugged her shoulders. "I didn't go out with you because you're rich."

Apollo lit a cigarette, took a few quick puffs, and put it out.

"I know. That's why I love you and trust you."

He took his clothes off. "Come on then. Shall I enter you or will you enter me?" he said while taking the plastic dildo out of its bag.

"I'll enter you," she said and ordered him to assume the prostrate position.

He handed her the dildo. She shook her head, "I want to feel you with my hand."

Apollo's eyes sparkled and widened in surprise. He prostrated himself without discussion. Ayn quickly took off her clothes, then washed her hands thoroughly with mineral water. She lightly slapped his ass a few times then pushed in a finger and pulled it out. Apollo turned onto his back and said to her, "My grandmother would do that to me when she concealed packets of drugs up my ass." Then he returned to his previous position.

Ayn resumed her task with the meticulousness of a sculptor. She inserted one finger, then two, then three, then the whole hand. She spread her five fingers inside him and pulled them out. Apollo wailed like a cat. Then he rolled onto his back and took a deep breath which he blew out forcefully. She saw a demonic look in his eyes and hesitation between the burning desire to abandon himself to her and the fear of her taking possession of him. Ayn hit him hard on the buttocks, and he reverted to the prone position. She inserted her hand in one go, and he screamed. She explored his ass and felt his intestines, as if seeing his ass from the inside. Then she gently worked her hand into his passage and crossed a gateway. Apollo held back his breaths. She passed through another narrower gateway and wormed her way deeper until half her arm was inside him. Then she pressed against the entrance to another threshold. Apollo screamed in terror, "Stop!" Ayn forced again and now she knew she could pluck his soul with her hand. He pushed her away and wept.

Ayn left him and went to the sea. She washed her hands clean, then slept on her own on the beach, completely exhausted.

Apollo woke Ayn up in the morning. "Ayn, come on. I have to go back to Dahab. Melissa wants me for something important."

"It's seven in the morning!" She got up and adjusted her clothing. "Who are you going to spend your birthday night with?"

As he was starting the car he said, "I don't know yet."

They went back to the café area on the seafront. Apollo left Ayn in one of the cafeterias by the sea and ordered her breakfast. He left, then came back to tell her where the party would be and added that Melissa would also be there. "She really hates you. Don't tell her that we sleep together." He shut up for a moment then said, "Or tell her. I don't care. I'm a free man."

At the party, a stout blonde woman engaged her in conversation with strained friendliness. She proudly introduced herself as one of the richest women in the world. Ayn mumbled, not being in the least bit interested in this trivial conversation. The woman continued chattering about herself until she mentioned Apollo's name. At this point Ayn showed some interest. More affectionately, as though they were two intimate friends, she told Ayn that she had written a letter to God asking Him to send her a man who fitted Apollo's description, and that she had sent the letter to God on the waves of the sea which then split to reveal Apollo carrying the letter. Ayn looked at the woman, who was over sixty-years old and said in her head, "Birds of a feather flock together." She took a crumpled piece of paper out of her bag and said, "Here's the letter if you don't believe me." Ayn responded in Arabic with a sarcastic tone, "I believe you, sister. I believe you." The woman was silent for a little while, then asked Ayn about her relationship with Apollo. Ayn replied cautiously, "We're friends." Then she asked directly, "Do you sleep with him?" Ayn dodged the question, "Apollo and I aren't in a relationship. I told you we were friends. Don't you understand English!" Then she got up, away from this juvenile old woman, and went to talk to other people.

She was observing Apollo, who had started to look drunk. He had begun to babble incoherently, if revealingly. All of a sudden he turned on the others and began to curse and punch anyone who tried to stop him, including Melissa. Ayn didn't know whether to get involved or not. But she made the mistake. She slapped Apollo in the face. He slapped her back harder, making Ayn sway on her feet. But before she fell over she grabbed Apollo by the hair and dragged him down with her to the ground where they kicked at each other. A policeman intervened to break up the fight.

Ayn got up from the floor and arranged her clothes while giving Apollo poisonous looks. The policeman asked her if she wanted to bring charges against Apollo. Ayn regained her composure and answered, "No, it's a family quarrel." The policeman showed his surprise as he looked at Ayn, with her clearly Egyptian features, and at Apollo, who was standing muttering in his own language, and asked her, "How so?" From his accent, Ayn determined he was Upper Egyptian, so she said they were brother and sister. The officer repeated his question with greater surprise. Ayn answered in a raised voice, her anger increasing, "From a different mother and father, pal. Is that strange?!" She left the party for the bus station, cursing the Corsican, and she swore not to see him again.

Ali finally invited her to dinner at his new home. Ayn asked him why he had moved. "The wife didn't like it," he answered in a neutral tone. Ayn felt that this was better, as she wouldn't have known how to behave in the house whose every corner had witnessed her love, her anger, and her pain. Perhaps that was what "the wife" hadn't liked either, given that she was well aware of Ayn and Ali's relationship. She had seen them together on that sad night, the night Ayn danced for herself, the night she revealed everything in her heart, and had gone.

Ayn bought red roses for Salma, and went to dinner accompanied by Aisha. Ali opened the door in the old pajama bottoms that Ayn knew well, and that he had often worn when it was chilly. She teased him while she took stock of his appearance, "You got married in your old clothes, Ali." He laughed and said, "And so? Don't you have a proverb that goes, 'If you lose your past, you're lost'?" Ayn smiled and didn't comment.

Then Salma came in. Ayn was disconcerted at seeing her, but kept control of her facial expression. Salma welcomed Ayn. They embraced warmly and sat down on separate chairs. Was this the woman Ayn had seen before? She didn't believe it. Was this the woman armed with the full battery of femininity? Sitting opposite her now was another woman. A calm woman, without makeup, wearing ordinary clothes that made plain her weight gain and didn't reveal any particular taste. A comfortable woman, a woman who'd gotten what she wanted.

Ayn decided to reflect on this change later. Now, she had to take part in the gathering lest her silence arouse suspicions. She directed her conversation at Ali. She told a few stories about Apollo while looking at Salma. She wanted to reassure her that she had another man. But she knew that her every particle radiated her love for Ali. Then she switched the discussion to public affairs so that Salma could join in. But she didn't join in and showed no interest in politics or society, which had always been the mainstay of Ayn and Ali's conversations. What did interest this woman who sat attentively filing her nails?

After dinner, they all went to Aisha's house for Ali and Salma's wedding party.

Salma sat at a distance from Ali because she didn't like smoke. Ayn sat next to him and smoked and drank whiskey with him. They talked about various things. When the flow of conversation hit a point of disagreement, Ayn laughed and asked Ali, "What do you talk about with Salma?" Ali laughed as he answered, "We don't talk at all." Ayn looked at Salma in an effort to read her. She shook her head and said to Ali, "She's . . . ." Ali lost control of himself and laughed in spite of himself, but he refrained from comment.

Rai music boomed out and the dancing began.

Salma gently led Ali off to dance with her. Ayn noticed that her movements had become more fluid. Ayn remained seated and considered the pair of them together. She tried to find anything in common between them. She couldn't. She looked at them again. Salma seemed happy. Ali, on the other hand . . . she didn't know exactly, but to her he seemed to be playing a role. The role of a husband who feels obliged to make his wife happy. There had been no such obligations between her and Ali. Both of them had behaved instinctively, according to their feelings.

Ayn got up to refresh her drink. Ali tenderly drew her over to dance with them. Ayn declined, but Ali insisted and pulled her over to his circle. Ayn discerned veiled anger on Salma's face. She danced a little with them then stepped back. She went to the bathroom and cried. She had been so touched by Ali's move. She didn't believe that he had pulled her over to dance with them. It was as though he had wanted to say to her that she was with him, that the fact he had gotten married did not mean she had been discarded. I love you Ali.

She filled her glass with some trepidation because she had started to feel the effects of the alcohol and was worried she might say something inappropriate. But what would she do if she didn't drink. She went back to her seat beside Ali. He was also glowing with love for her. Every part of him spoke love for her. She was embarrassed and got up saying she would chat a little with Salma.

She sat down by Salma and took her hand. "Salma . . . ." But she didn't know what she wanted to say to her. So Salma talked and said what Ayn had never expected to hear from her, "I know that you're in love with Ali." Ayn looked at her in embarrassment then said, "Ali is a lovely person. If you love him faithfully, he'll meet love with love." Then she asked her, "Do you love him, Salma?" She answered yes. Despite herself, Ayn's tears started to flow as she said, "Love him more." Salma turned her face away, so Ayn turned herself toward her and said to her with all honesty, "If you really love Ali, I can love you like my sister." But Salma kept her face averted.

Subsequently, Salma would refuse to be her friend. She accused Ayn behind her back of having kissed Ali on the mouth in front of her and not having shown consideration for her feelings. Ali would say he didn't remember because he had had too much to drink. Ayn would deny that she had done this. She would tell Ali that Salma had gotten angry when he included her in their dance, because she didn't want the presence of another woman sharing him with her. Which was her right. But there had been no need to make false accusations. "Give her some time," Ali said. Time, however, would only confirm the truth of Ayn's words. Salma totally rejected her.

Perhaps if Ali had treated her coldly, or if Ayn had felt a change in his heart, she might have kept away. She might have changed the way she felt too. But what happened was that they became tender in the way they treated each other, and the tension that had occasionally embittered their relationship disappeared. True, Ayn sometimes bitterly reproached Ali and cried, or burst out with her love, which she described as absolute and unconditional, and how she wanted nothing from him in return. True, she had been impudent and reminded Ali of his old words about his need for freedom and his hatred of being chained down. How he had accused her of having taken possession of him, only for him to leave her and place himself in a silk-lined cage with a bird who didn't know how to fly. While she, who truly extolled freedom, had torn the ties from her shroud and soared in spaces she had not known before and plunged to depths no one before her had reached. Depths whose existence we have learned to deny or totally ignore when we discover them, so that in the view of other, sane people we don't appear crazy or criminal or perverted. All of this made Ali wish not to meet Ayn and to avoid her confrontations. Still these occasions were limited and only happened when Ayn got drunk. In the end, Ali didn't, in seriousness, want not to see her, and enjoyed her endless arguing. He was also in love with her. And after all, he was a man made happy by a woman's love for him.

This, perhaps, was what made Ayn move forward with her relationship with Apollo against her intuition that it would end in disaster. Ali would go home to his country for good after a few months, his wife would bear him a baby boy or girl, and he would be distracted from her, perhaps forget her. What would she do with this love that accumulated and circled her pain?

Was it a sign?

Did her impulse to change the direction of her journey hold some significance?

She had a passion for examining the signs and interpreting the coincidences which followed one another in a pattern that couldn't be subjected to the random logic usually characteristic of coincidence.

She had another passion that clashed with the logic of subjecting signs to a deductive reading: to follow her feelings.

The plan was for Ayn to go to Siwa with Apollo and his Korean friend, Hyun Yu, whose name meant 'Fire in the Darkness.' This was after Apollo had come to Cairo, to make amends for what he had ruined on the night of his birthday and, also, to meet this friend and former fellow prisoner.

After much nonsense and mutual recrimination between Ayn and Apollo, of which the Korean had understood nothing, Ayn agreed to go with them on a condition that she whispered into his ear. Apollo laughed and said to her, "If you had been patient, I would have offered him to you myself." Then he whispered in her ear that his friend had been suffering from a problem since getting out of prison: he hadn't been able to have a relationship with a woman. "I can't believe you read my mind." The pair of them laughed together, and Hyun, who had somehow understood that the talk was about him, joined in. Ayn looked at Hyun in amazement. This was the tallest Korean she had ever seen. True, she hadn't seen every Korean, but this one was more than six feet tall. His face resembled those carved in Buddhist temples that she had only seen in photographs. She hadn't yet tried East Asia, and dealt with the subject as cross-cultural exchange.

Ayn changed her mind, however, when they were on the 26th July Corridor out of Cairo. "Stop the car," she commanded Apollo, who looked at her in surprise. "I'm not going to Siwa." Apollo pulled over at the side of the road. "I don't understand you," he said nervously. Ayn repeated her words, "I tell you I'm not going." She got out of the car, which took off furiously.

In Lebanon Square she took a cab to the Sinai bus station and bought a ticket to Saint Catherine.

The bus turned up late and in need of repair. Ayn and the rest of the passengers waited an hour until another bus came.

Not an auspicious start.

There were about fifteen passengers, six of whom got out at Suez. The bus set off again, with a strong smell of smoke emanating from the front.

"Driver, there's a smell of smoke," shouted one of the passengers from the rear.

The driver ignored him. The passenger advanced toward him and shouted again. The driver responded that it was the gear lever. "What gear lever?" whispered the other passengers.

Some distance after the Suez Canal tunnel, but before Moses' Springs, the smell of smoke grew worse and filled the whole bus. The engine gave a last gasp and died.

The passengers filed slowly out of the bus and stood venting their frustrations by the side of the road. The driver and ticket collector lifted the cover over the engine and stuck their heads inside. "The drive's gone."

"What a nightmare."

A number of attempts to repair the engine with primitive tools led, in the end, to the bus moving one hundred yards, only to come to a final halt.

They got out again, swearing and cursing at the East Delta Bus Company.

Ayn sat on the sand and thought that the breakdown was Apollo's doing. Or Ali's, whom she had called and told where she was going. She was going to climb the mountain and speak to the Lord to petition Him with a particular request which Ali knew all about. Ayn felt that the two men had, each in his own way, conspired together to ruin her trip.

By chance, there was a mechanic among the passengers. He generously volunteered his efforts, which he had withheld at the first stoppage, and helped the driver and ticket collector. Further efforts began, during which three passengers for Abu Rudeis found alternative means of transport.

These stubborn efforts were crowned with success when the bus finally spluttered to life to the accompaniment of whoops and praises. In delight at this turn of events, the remaining passengers shared food and juice among themselves. Owing to their small number and the exceptional circumstances the driver allowed them to smoke on the bus. He replayed the video of "al-Limbi" on the request of one of the passengers who had been asleep the first time round.

They finally arrived at Saint Catherine. But Ayn's fancy changed again and she decided to return to Cairo and catch up with Apollo in Siwa.

On the first day, Apollo fulfilled Ayn's condition for coming to Siwa. When he saw the resentment on her face, he intervened with his own penis. Ayn never expected that this tall Korean would have such a small penis. It was tinier than her finger. She left the two of them to play with her body, but she didn't feel the arousal that she often felt in her imagination. "Enough," she said, pushing them away with her legs. They lifted their heads toward her questioningly. "The game's over." She got up. The two men looked at each other and burst out laughing while they repeated Ayn's words. She also joined in the laughter.

On the second day, Apollo would challenge a jinn. He would place a small rock in the road for the driver's side wheels to go over, and take off at high speed. The jinn would either kill him or become his slave. Ayn would be carried along by Apollo's fancies. Perhaps she was carried along by the dark part of herself, by her demon. The sensible Korean would refuse to participate. But he would stand by the edge of the road, like a linesman in a game of soccer.

Apollo, in the driving seat, took off in an ardent search for illusory answers to existential questions. Ayn, next to him, was encroaching on the darkness in her heart. Apollo won the bet, and the car did not overturn.

In the small hotel where they were staying, Ayn asked Apollo if he wanted her to penetrate him. He shook his head no. "I prefer to die in my own way," he replied. Then he asked her if she would like him to penetrate her. She said yes. He did it, but he failed to reach the circle of her pain, and was unable to liberate the part that she had grown used to liberating through him.

On the third day, Hyun stood at the side of the road, and Ayn hesitated about riding the car when she looked deeply into Apollo's eyes. "Come on. Don't you want to be free of pain forever?" Apollo said, looking with the same intensity into Ayn's eyes. But he didn't wait for her answer. He played the song "My Way" at full volume and took off one last time at top speed.

Ayn would see the headlights hurled through the darkness. She would hear her screams intersecting a single scream that penetrated the noise of the car's metal: "I," as it bounced, "Did," on the asphalt, "It," once, "Myyy," twice, "Waaay," three times. Ayn, who could feel her heart thumping against her ribs, would run with Hyun as fast as they could to reach where the car had rolled one last time and righted itself; Frank Sinatra had gone quiet. The doors were open and Apollo was bent over the steering wheel.

She raised up his face and burst out laughing. Apollo had stuck his long tongue out at the jinn. His sense of victory was etched on his open eyes. He hadn't lost a tooth. There wasn't a scratch on him, not a single drop of blood. Ayn didn't notice that her laughter had turned into wailing until Hyun grabbed her and pulled her away from the car. Still, she went back and took Apollo's tongue in her mouth and said the words that Apollo had always pressed her to say. Now that he was dead, she said them freely, "I love you Apollo."

"What shall we do now? Do we inform the police or bury him here?" asked Hyun Yu.

"Apollo wanted to be cremated," replied Ayn as she remembered an old wish of his, "and his ashes scattered over the Red Sea at Dahab."

"But he chose to die here. Don't you think so?"

Ayn pondered for a minute, then said, "Yeah. I think he wanted to die here." She remembered the last sentence he had said to her. Had he wanted her with him. Had she wanted to go with him. Ayn sighed and said, "Let's dig his grave here. At least he won't be alone, he'll be among the dead who inhabit this mountain."

They started to dig with their hands. Then they went to the car to look for anything that would help them dig. They broke off the metal sheet that was hanging off the back of the car and resumed their task. Ayn laughed all of a sudden and Hyun asked her why. Ayn waved the piece of metal in the air and said, "Apollo really loved asses, and here we are digging his grave with a piece of the rear-end of a car."

They finished digging the grave shortly before dawn. Ayn kissed Apollo again on his mouth, and they placed him in the grave. Ayn remembered the plastic dildo that never left Apollo's side. She went back to the car and took it out of its bag. She placed it between his thighs and said, after having ensured everything was perfect, "Now let's fill it in."

They shoveled earth into the hole. Hyun marked the site by writing Apollo's name in Korean characters at the foot of the Mountain of the Dead. Then, with difficulty, they extracted their things from what remained of the car and set off on foot for the bus station like two lost ghosts.

5.

To whom should Ayn turn when she reached Cairo cloaked in the dust of Apollo's grave? The question did not occur to Ayn. She had lost the ability to think. She hadn't eaten or slept in two days. Hyun, who had remained to a degree conscious, rolled her along like a small rock from one bus to another and from one bus station to another until they reached Cairo. At that point Ayn started moving to a different rhythm and with a different sensibility and, intentionally or unintentionally, slipped out of Hyun's arms.

Now she knew her way. The way she had ascended hundreds, perhaps thousands, of times only for her to run away and begin again. Ayn carried her past and present and laid them at Ali's door.

Siwa, Apollo, a wager, a jinn, a car, a rock. A grave. Dead. Ayn ranted deliriously in Ali's arms, whose eyes filled with tears when he saw her in such a state. He carried her to the couch in the room adjacent to his office, and covered her with his jacket. She clung to his hand, and he lay down next to her with anxiety and fear riveted in his eyes. He waited for her to come round and from time to time he listened to her heartbeat that raced and then dropped so low he thought she was dead. He looked at her face whose innocence and naughtiness, and even anger, enraptured him. He saw phantoms struggling above her contorted features. Ali was lying next to her at a loss. He did not know what to do. Should he call a doctor? Should he order food? Should he pour some whiskey down her throat? Should he sleep with her?

His wife called. He told her perfunctorily that he had work to do and would be late. As he was hanging up, he started thinking practically again. He ordered grilled meat, soup, and various salads from the kebab restaurant that Ayn liked. He remained sitting at his desk looking at Ayn across the distance between them. He shook his head while thinking about why Ayn did to herself what she did. Was he the reason? Or was it the madness that occasionally took possession of her. He remembered how she had taken off into the Great Sahara without thought, without plan, and without visas. He remembered what she had said when she was at the airport in Algeria. He smiled despite the anxiety. But this was a different madness. This time she had topped his wildest imaginings, even though he had often expected ill results from her relationship with Apollo. In a certain way, Ali felt guilty. True, he had repeatedly warned her. But he felt responsible for her, despite his repeated denials of this. He went back over to Ayn, and gently held her hand. Ayn felt his touch and opened her clouded eyes. She felt his wedding ring and pushed his left hand away. Ali placed his rejected hand on his leg as if it were not his own limb. She closed her eyes again and did not open them until Ali whispered into her ear. He raised her up slightly and propped her head against the armrest of the couch so he could feed her. He filled the spoon with meat broth and put it to her lips. Ayn swallowed the soup with difficulty. But she gradually felt better; she sat up straighter and asked for some meat. Ali thanked God in a low voice. Only then did he feel some relief.

Then with an eerie calm, Ayn told him everything that had happened. It was as if she were speaking about other people, or telling Ali, as she used to do, the plot of a novel she had read. Ali listened and didn't interrupt her. Perhaps he had nothing to say. Only when she had finished the story did Ali sigh deeply and say, "Thank God you're okay." But in fact, he wasn't sure that Ayn was okay. Physically yes, but mentally he didn't know. She had just told the story with bewildering calm, as if under the influence of drugs or hypnosis. Without meaning to, he found himself asking her if she was taking any kind of drugs. She shook her head.

After some hesitation, Ali told her that he had to go home, and he pointed to the wedding ring that squeezed his finger. Ayn noticed that his finger had gotten fatter, and that the ring was stuck to it since it would be impossible to remove without cutting the finger off. She shrugged her shoulders; some of her strength had returned. He asked her whether she wanted to stay in the office and sleep there until the morning, or whether he should give her a lift to her house. She would stay in the office.

"The rest of the food is in the fridge. There's whiskey in the desk drawer if you feel like a drink." He produced a spare key to the door and said, "Lock the door after I go, but don't leave it in the lock." Then he added, "Or if you want to go out for any reason. Just don't forget the key." She nodded.

She walked him to the door. "I'll call you from home to check you're okay." She locked the door behind him. She sat in front of the television and followed the moving images in front of her without seeing anything until she fell asleep where she sat.

Ayn regained consciousness in the morning and looked around. She was in Ali's office. She looked at the dust stuck to her clothes, and remembered. But at the same time, she did not acknowledge the line dividing reality from dream, which had so blurred together that she no longer knew where she was. She remembered details of her relationship with Apollo as though they were episodes from one of her epic dreams that she would watch and participate in while asleep in Ali's arms.

She went to the bathroom, undressed, and shook out her clothes. Then she washed her body and hair. She returned to the office and watched the succession of images on the television until Ali arrived.

She heard the key turning in the door, and ran to him and hung round his neck. Ali smiled to see her girlish mischief had come back. He handed her some juice and chocolate he had brought for her. She was happy and bounced around like a child, holding a carton of juice in one hand and chocolate bar in the other.

She sat on his knee as she used to and chattered away. Suddenly the ghost of Apollo appeared on her face, and her eyes filled with tears and her voice was choked. Ali asked her the question that had long kept him awake, "Did you love him?" in a voice of someone frightened of the question in case the answer shocked him. Ayn answered in confusion, "I don't know. I think so, perhaps, yes. I said it to him when he was dead, but I don't know if I said it in reaction or because

I felt it. But I think a part of me loved him, the dark part of me, or perhaps the enlightened part of me as he would say. I loved him as a person, I don't know, we were very similar, more than needed perhaps. But I didn't feel the real happiness with him that I felt when I was with you, in your arms when we were sleeping next to each other."

Ali turned to the computer. He didn't want to confront her now. Perhaps he had expected Ayn to deny she had loved that man in unambiguous terms, but she was reluctant. But didn't this reluctance mean she wasn't confident of her feelings. Ali swiveled to the side looking for the packet of cigarettes. He lit one and decided to start work, because he didn't like to think about these things. Ayn read the thoughts that Ali had refused to keep thinking. She clasped him round the shoulders and kissed him on the cheek. Then she whispered in his left ear, "I didn't love anyone but you, Ali." Without looking at her, he said with warmth, "Ayn, I have to work." Ayn stood up straight and said, "I also have to go home and change my clothes." She handed the spare key back to him, kissed him again, and left.

Ayn and Ali continued to meet at the office and the nearby bar. Ayn only remembered Salma's existence when she got hungry while drinking and Ali ordered dinner for her without joining her. "I'll have dinner at home," he would say as a fact to which he had adjusted. Ayn would lose her desire to eat and poke fun at Ali's tone, "How's the wife?" He would answer with more or less the same tone, "What's it got to do with you?" Ayn would raise the left corner of her mouth dismissively and say, "I'm just checking whether the Lord has breathed a soul into her yet or not."

This continued until Ali told her that another person would take over his post at work and that he would return home in a few weeks' time. Ayn was afflicted by her old confusion. This time, however, she didn't squander the remaining time quarreling. There was no longer enough time for dismay, reproach, and making up, which might swallow up the days left. Equally, nothing remained that called for quarreling. She loved him, that was all. She enjoyed the times she spent with him and stored up the smallest details. The time was approaching when she would recall these details and live on them for years to come. Sometimes they would stop meeting or calling each other. This was not out of anger or deliberately, but out of the fear that the feelings that Ali's hesitation unconsciously expressed and that Ayn, even when silent, could not always hide because her body radiated them, would come out into the open.

She hated the Salah Salem expressway, the road to the airport. The whole way, Ayn clung to Ali's arm. She had insisted on taking him after he had told her that his wife had departed the week before. If only the president were to decide to go out now, closing the roads for hours, and the plane were to take off without Ali. What would happen? He would stay behind for a day or two and take the next plane. One or two days would be like the five minutes she used to ask him for so that he would stay next to her while they were waking up. Were, Ayn reminded herself.

"Ali . . . ."

He turned to her.

"Don't be a stranger."

"I will come back. I've got a return ticket."

The word 'return' rang in her ears. Return to here or to there; which was home? Her mind slipped away from the present moment and she called to mind words closely and historically associated with 'return.' The return of the Palestinian refugees, the right of return, the return of the

Lebanese exiles. There was also the return of the Sudanese refugees, the Iraqis, Egyptians, and others. She let out a laugh and Ali asked her why. She told him all the associations of the word 'return' she had been thinking about. He smiled.

Then she said to him, "All of that because you said 'return ticket.' If you had said, for example, 'round-trip ticket,' none of those ideas would have occurred to me." They shared a laugh. Then Ayn fell silent until they reached the airport. In the Departure Lounge they stood face to face.

"Ali, I want to say something . . . "

"Go on."

"I don't love you . . ."

Ali smiled, "Really?"

"I breathe you."

Ali didn't know how to respond to these words. He thought about saying something like, "But I'm polluted air." But he didn't and opted for silence.

"I'm being serious. I breathe you. Please don't be a stranger."

"I'll be back, Ayn. Don't you say that whoever drinks from the Nile always comes back?"

"Yes, or they get bilharzia, and come back for treatment."

Ali burst out laughing along with Ayn until her eyes filled with tears.

They embraced with true love, pure love.

Perhaps that was what had to be. And it was. Ayn thought, having resumed her habit of talking to Ali internally:

To live the experience together. So we might know. Since how would we have acquired this knowledge if we hadn't given it a try. It was necessary that you got married, Ali, you had to try the institution for yourself, with your critical mind. You had to live that life, if it's possible to truly call it life, completely and not halfheartedly, in order to discover with your heart what your mind couldn't let you know. It had to be. For you to discover that maybe you weren't a traditionalist through and through, and that I'm not mad through and through. That what is lacking in you is completed in me, that what is lacking in me is completed in you.

It had to be. Living the experience with you and without you. Being conscious of what it means for you to be wed to another who doesn't compare to me. I'm not the competitive kind, you know that. Passing below where you worked and not going up. Hearing a joke or news I wanted to share and restraining myself and putting down the phone whenever I was about to call.

I'm talking to you now internally. I invoke the images of you inscribed in my imagination in their different moods. That's not too bad now.

Distance is no problem as long as reunion is not far off. I have asked God not to extend our separation, if that is good for you and me. My heart tells me that you are mine, of me, and with me, and that I am yours, of you, and with you.

I'm not going to hurry myself, or you.

The time will come when we don't have to call for a few minutes, when we don't meet briefly and nervously. The time will come when we will sip each other's nectar at leisure. Nectar that revives us and never fills us. You know how I never have enough of you. The time will come.

There is a promise between us.

Until that time came, Ayn would be occupied with a number of research topics for various bodies, and would participate in a number of conferences in various countries. Ayn knew that the recommendations of these studies would not be adopted and that the only benefit she would derive would be the material returns or the opportunities for foreign travel. She kept in telephone contact with Ali. These conversations swung between joy and anger. Ayn got enraged when she asked him how things were and he replied fine or comfortable. Ayn would demand, "Why are you fine?!" as if Ali should have been sad, upset, or troubled. She was happy when she told him that she missed him and he replied with that dirty word that had become her proof of his love, which he was unable to express openly except through this word. Between anger and joy, Ayn decided at least one hundred times to stop calling Ali and get to know other men, to give herself another chance to love. To start her life over again.

But Ayn would never behave like a woman who wanted to end a relationship and start her life over again. Ayn would behave like a woman infatuated with love, and with the eternal.

Ayn got angry with Ali during a phone call and, on the same day, she became acquainted with an Austrian sociologist at a conference in Vienna. She spent the night with him, but without any real pleasure, despite Johann's tenderness and his sexual expertise. She turned him down when he asked her whether he could spend the next night with her. Ayn, after all, felt sick of men in general, and never thought it good to sleep with the same man twice, except rarely. The only man who didn't induce this sickness was Ali, who had gotten married in the end and left her. The anger built up inside her, and this Austrian ignited it when he described her as only wanting one-night stands. "And what do you want?" she screamed down the telephone that communicated between the hotel rooms. He put the phone down on her after having called her a slut. Her eyes widened in astonishment and she opened her mouth to answer him, but the bastard had hung up. She had wanted to tell him that that was what men do, so why get angry with women when they do the same thing. She decided to teach him a lesson in the morning, and perhaps slap him in retaliation for his rudeness. But he apologized to her at the breakfast table. Ayn insisted on her revenge by repeating her delayed response from the night before. He apologized again and said that he didn't like such behavior in men or woman alike. Ayn looked at him warily.

A few weeks after the conference ended, Ayn was surprised to receive a call from Johann in Cairo. She didn't recall having given him her number, but he told her that the details of all the conference participants were available on the organizers' website. Ayn remembered the one night she had spent with him, how he had been tender with her, actually more tender than was warranted in a one-night stand. But she had no objections to exploring Cairo and Alexandria with him, and they spent other nights together.

Ayn's problem was that she understood that much of her behavior in her relationships with men was conditioned by her relationship with Ali. She wouldn't have gone so far in her relationship with Johann unless she had felt that Ali, as he said, was settled into his new life. She displayed a great deal of kindness and concern for Johann; he cascaded her with gushing emotions, which was something she was unaccustomed to. She had frequently blamed Ali for stinting in the expression of his feelings but now she felt that that would be far better than this sentimental excess. Ayn enjoyed herself to a certain extent the first week. But she had rapidly started to feel bored with the onset of week two. She didn't know how to react to all these gushing emotions, to a man the same age as her behaving like a teenager. Then his vacation came to an end and he returned to work. Ayn thought the subject was over and done with. But he sent her three or four emails every day, most of which she didn't answer.

It seems that a policy of indifference makes a man more passionate about a woman.

She told Ali about Johann and about everything that had happened. His voice on the phone was neutral, even at points encouraging. If only he'd forbid her this relationship, as he had done before, but it wasn't his right. He knew that well. He had warned her about Apollo because from his perspective he was a criminal. But Johann, he was her social and intellectual equal. Ayn began praising Johann's character to disguise her anger from Ali.

Johann invited her to visit him. She declined on the pretext that it was very difficult for Egyptians to obtain European visas, especially if it wasn't for some official reason. She didn't know whether his offer to marry her so she could obtain a European passport granting her freedom to travel was a joke or in earnest. Still, she thanked him for his generous offer and sacrificed a European passport. After a few more weeks of passionate emails, Johann would repeat his offer of marriage to Ayn. She was confused by this man who wrote poetry to her. She remembered her resolutions to start her life over again. But she was hesitant. She imposed impossible conditions on the marriage—she wouldn't have children, she wouldn't live in Austria, she would have the right to initiate a divorce, she would be completely free because she had another lover—so that he would turn her down. In this way, she soothed her conscience. But, amazingly, he accepted. Ayn decided that this man had to be a head case. What else could make him accept such an unfair marriage?

She stopped answering his messages and changed her phone number.

Then Ali came on his summer vacation, which he used to spend in his country. Ayn was very happy to see him. She clung to his neck and breathed him in. He was also happy to see her and carried her in his arms laughing. But she felt that there was something missing. There was something Ali had lost over there. Ayn walked round him, feeling him, contemplating him. The eleven-year-old boy had gotten lost. Ali had grown up. His soul had aged.

Ayn was dumbfounded. She felt intense loathing for his wife. She didn't know whether Ali could perceive it or not. She didn't know whether to confront him or not. He asked her the reason for her silence, and she became confused. She spoke guardedly. But, in the end, Ali was her friend. And friendship is based on honesty: one should be honest with one's friend in what one says and does. She asked him with a tender sadness about the boy he had been. He turned his face away from her eyes, away from her voice, away from everything she represented to him and reminded him of.

The encounter began to warn of the dangers of distance. Ayn saw hesitation cutting across the wrinkles scored by the years of his life and deepened by his marriage to that woman. Ayn tried to avoid the confrontation as much as she could, for she well knew what the result would be. Yet her desire to restore the lost boy drove her on. She confronted him. He withdrew. He closed in on himself like a sea anemone when it feels something threatening approach.

Ayn's anxiety grew. She didn't know what to do. She was apprehensive, but Ali's silence forced her to withdraw. She went home and curled up in bed. She hid from herself. She cried. She went over what she had said to him. She went over his silence. Her certainty grew.

He wouldn't see. Or refused to see. Or saw and did not want to admit he saw.

Ali left without saying goodbye. Without a word. Like a stranger. He fled.

Ayn was defeated.

Had he resolved things for good? Had the circle been completed and closed?

Ayn asked herself this, feeling bitterness and sadness the likes of which she had not felt before. The pain went beyond its boundaries this time, and deepened the wounds that hadn't healed. What was he running away from? From her or from himself? If his feelings for her had waned or changed, he would have confronted her and not run away. Had he come to realize the error of his rational decision to marry that woman, and didn't know how to untie the knot with the minimum of psychological and social damage? Was he still vacillating between his old desire for freedom—and closeness to Ayn made him aware of the enormity of his loss—and his desire for traditional, settled, married life? He had often talked about the split personality endured by the eastern man, in particular, and he was one of them. He was afraid he might break the limits, or cross them, and that his wife would act likewise: he would never accept that, in spite of his theoretical belief in equal rights for men and women. But the only thing Ayn cared about was his happiness, which she saw he had lost for good with this marriage. She didn't necessarily intend that he divorce his wife and marry her. Ayn didn't want a traditional bond. Ayn wanted him to be free, for himself first and then for her. To what extent would Ali remain prisoner to his split personality? And for how long would he waste the moments that fate might not grant again?

Ayn hadn't called him, and he hadn't initiated a call.

She spent five months caught between waiting for the man of her life and piteous attempts to run away from him. With each passing day her confidence crumbled. Her misery extended until the night of the full moon of their anniversary month. Ayn gave herself to the moon and asked God to turn her heart away from love for Ali if there was no good in it for her. In the night, she was visited by Noor, the mutual friend at whose house she had first met Ali. "I looked for you everywhere. Ali sent me to make sure you were okay." This was the sign; this was the good news.

She called him without hesitation. His voice came warm and welcoming. Her doubts evaporated, and her voice strained in excitement. Ali asked for her news. "Waiting," she answered in one word. Then she reproached him for his distance. "You left, Ayn, and I was dismayed." Ali reproached her with a sweetness that made her remember how she had gathered her things, how she had left the food she had prepared, and how she had gone from the house he had rented, leaving behind her severe anxiety. She remembered how many times she had left. She remembered the words, 'Just leave' that she had said to Ali, and his response. But she was the one who had left. She was the one who had suggested separating. She was the one who had swung between drawing close and drawing away. This man had been tortured so much by her indecision, made so miserable by her love.

Reproach ended and bitterness passed. Their easy conversations of before resumed.

Ayn decided to visit Ali in his country, and told him this in another call. He made her welcome and smoothed the visa process for her. She bought the plane ticket and packed her bag. The morning of departure she changed her mind. She called Ali to inform him that she wouldn't be coming. He asked her in surprise the reason why. "I'm scared I'll get hurt, Ali."

As great as her longing to see Ali and her desire to make him happy, even if only by spending an hour with him telling jokes and funny stories, equally great was her fear of his causing her further emotional pain. She no longer had the emotional reserves to handle the pain. Ayn would never be able to stop her outpouring of feelings for Ali, and he would be unable to handle this outpour, and would take refuge in the barrier of silence that only confirmed his love for Ayn. On previous occasions the suffering had caught up with her, even if this was unintentional. This time she was afraid she would lead herself directly to the pain. There was his wife and his child, of whose birth Ali had not dared tell Ayn, a child that Ayn would love as her own without seeing. Perhaps there was a sense of contentment, stability, or comfort. Their being together, the lover and the wife, in the same place would make Ali aware once again of what he had lost. Then he would set down boundaries and shut the gates, in spite of himself, before Ayn. He would hurt her in self-defense. No she would never do that. She had promised herself not to expose herself ever again to such pain. Ayn would not go. She would wait for him to come.

She would wait. Because she had discovered that the more she tried to escape him, the more she would grow close. She would wait. Because she knew his little finger was worth the world. When she had told Ali this, she had meant what she said and not intended to be rhetorical or high-flown. She had only been stating a fact. She had known many other men and hid nothing from Ali. The simplicity and spontaneity with which she said these words in the middle of her stories about other men had made Ali look at her deeply in shock and love. This woman disarmed him. And in his being disarmed was his highest strength.

6.

Ali will come, and go
and come and go.
Each time I will ask him
till when will you stay in this middle ground?
till when will you stay on the border
between here and there?
each time he'll turn his face to other grounds
not here not there
and say, We never met each other
I'll shake my head in denial and say, Don't be
    a stranger
each time I'll ask myself when will he really come
    back to me
and I wait.

Until he returns
wholeheartedly
and pierces my inner being, whose being touched
    stopped ages ago
the longing of years slips away
and tears of joy free from pain fall
my soul trembles as if uniting with the Holy Spirit.
My moans break and my sobbing rises
he enfolds me inside us
I willingly give my soul up to him.

Then he goes.
Did he really return?
Is the return here or there?
I'm afraid that here is the illusion, there the truth

But he returns.
Here. To me.

He surrenders himself to me
and entrusts me with his soul
and touches my womb from the beginning
and my longing slips away in spite of me
and the pain suppressed inside me is liberated
my historic pain that I've borne for ages
I tremble the tremendum of a soul uniting with the
    Holy Spirit.

Ali will come, and go
Each time I will say to him
here is where I want to be
in your arms
all life long, and after.

Ali will come, and go
Each time I will say to him
if I die now
I would be content
that I lived by your love
and remained faithful to you alone.

Then
the news will come to her sleeping
when she is in his arms
people assembling from all directions
asking about the prophet's spouse
other people indicate from afar
there
she is still shepherding her wilderness
they advance shyly
she lifts her eyes toward them
she reads the news in the confused faces
before one of them utters it
the prophet is dead.

She wakes from her sleep and feels the two arms that
    have started to get cold
the news is still echoing in her ears
the prophet is dead.

She doesn't scoop dust onto her hair
she doesn't rend her robe or beat her chest
she extracts herself from two arms now totally cold
she stands up
and decides to start over again.

٧.

A woman dwelling by the grave of her man
wearing a white robe and waiting for
moonrise
scatters violet petals in the morning
and asks the Lord in the evening:
Has the time not yet come?
It hasn't yet come
a long time
a long, long time
one night, its moon grown full
and illumining his grave
the man came out smiling
young like he hadn't been
he held the hand of a woman
her face illumined and she smiled
young like she hadn't been.

Epilogue

Writing has no mercy for father or mother or lover. I find myself in agreement now with Roland Barthes. I hadn't known that the novel is a living creature with the capacity to grow and develop according to its own conditions until I had started to write myself. Writing is only subject to its own conditions and desires. I attempted, as much as I could, to keep away from any social or political context that might ruin the sense of love.

I prefaced this novel with a dedication to the beloved. But according to Barthes the novel may in the end smother the beloved and only exalt the writing self. Even so I must give credit to Ali. If this person had not entered my life, if I had not loved him, and he loved me, to such a degree, it would not have been possible to write this novel. I don't know precisely whether I dedicate this novel to Ali, the man I love, or the imaginary Ali of the novel. The two characters are intertwined to a degree that it is hard for me to disentangle. The dedication is not important in the end.

I love you, Ali. And I love my self because my self loves you.

I thank you for the life you gave me in reality and in the imagination.

And I thank you for Warda: I dreamed of a baby girl, and she arrived as a novel.

Ayn al-Saqi

Modern Arabic Literature
from the American University in Cairo Press

Bahaa Abdelmegid *Saint Theresa* and *Sleeping with Strangers*
Ibrahim Abdel Meguid *Birds of Amber* • *Distant Train*
No One Sleeps in Alexandria • *The Other Place*
Yahya Taher Abdullah *The Collar and the Bracelet*
The Mountain of Green Tea
Leila Abouzeid *The Last Chapter*
Hamdi Abu Golayyel *A Dog with No Tail* • *Thieves in Retirement*
Yusuf Abu Rayya *Wedding Night*
Ahmed Alaidy *Being Abbas el Abd*
Idris Ali *Dongola* • *Poor*
Radwa Ashour *Granada* • *Specters*
Ibrahim Aslan *The Heron* • *Nile Sparrows*
Alaa Al Aswany *Chicago* • *Friendly Fire* • *The Yacoubian Building*
Fadhil al-Azzawi *Cell Block Five* • *The Last of the Angels*
The Traveler and the Innkeeper
Ali Bader *Papa Sartre*
Liana Badr *The Eye of the Mirror*
Hala El Badry *A Certain Woman* • *Muntaha*
Salwa Bakr *The Golden Chariot* • *The Man from Bashmour*
The Wiles of Men
Halim Barakat *The Crane*
Hoda Barakat *Disciples of Passion* • *The Tiller of Waters*
Mourid Barghouti *I Saw Ramallah*
Mohamed Berrada *Like a Summer Never to Be Repeated*
Mohamed El-Bisatie *Clamor of the Lake* • *Drumbeat*
Houses Behind the Trees • *Hunger* • *Over the Bridge*
Mahmoud Darwish *The Butterfly's Burden*
Tarek Eltayeb *Cities without Palms*
Mansoura Ez Eldin *Maryam's Maze*
Ibrahim Farghali *The Smiles of the Saints*
Hamdy el-Gazzar *Black Magic*
Randa Ghazy *Dreaming of Palestine*
Gamal al-Ghitani *Pyramid Texts* • *The Zafarani Files* • *Zayni Barakat*
Tawfiq al-Hakim *The Essential Tawfiq al-Hakim*
Yahya Hakki *The Lamp of Umm Hashim*
Abdelilah Hamdouchi *The Final Bet*
Bensalem Himmich *The Polymath* • *The Theocrat*
Taha Hussein *The Days*
Sonallah Ibrahim *Cairo: From Edge to Edge* • *The Committee* • *Zaat*
Yusuf Idris *City of Love and Ashes* • *The Essential Yusuf Idris*
Denys Johnson-Davies *The AUC Press Book of Modern Arabic Literature* • *Homecoming*
In a Fertile Desert • *Under the Naked Sky*
Said al-Kafrawi *The Hill of Gypsies*
Sahar Khalifeh *The End of Spring*
The Image, the Icon, and the Covenant • *The Inheritance*

Edwar al-Kharrat *Rama and the Dragon • Stones of Bobello*
Betool Khedairi *Absent*
Mohammed Khudayyir *Basrayatha*
Ibrahim al-Koni *Anubis • Gold Dust • The Puppet • The Seven Veils of Seth*
Naguib Mahfouz *Adrift on the Nile • Akhenaten: Dweller in Truth*
Arabian Nights and Days • Autumn Quail • Before the Throne • The Beggar
The Beginning and the End • Cairo Modern
The Cairo Trilogy: Palace Walk, Palace of Desire, Sugar Street
Children of the Alley • The Coffeehouse • The Day the Leader Was Killed
The Dreams • Dreams of Departure • Echoes of an Autobiography
The Essential Naguib Mahfouz • The Final Hour • The Harafish • Heart of the Night
In the Time of Love • The Journey of Ibn Fattouma • Karnak Café
Khan al-Khalili • Khufu's Wisdom • Life's Wisdom • Love in the Rain • Midaq Alley
The Mirage • Miramar • Mirrors • Morning and Evening Talk
Naguib Mahfouz at Sidi Gaber • Respected Sir • Rhadopis of Nubia
The Search • The Seventh Heaven • Thebes at War
The Thief and the Dogs • The Time and the Place
Voices from the Other World • Wedding Song
Mohamed Makhzangi *Memories of a Meltdown*
Alia Mamdouh *The Loved Ones • Naphtalene*
Selim Matar *The Woman of the Flask*
Ibrahim al-Mazini *Ten Again*
Yousef Al-Mohaimeed *Munira's Bottle • Wolves of the Crescent Moon*
Ahlam Mosteghanemi *Chaos of the Senses • Memory in the Flesh*
Shakir Mustafa *Contemporary Iraqi Fiction: An Anthology*
Mohamed Mustagab *Tales from Dayrut*
Buthaina Al Nasiri *Final Night*
Ibrahim Nasrallah *Inside the Night*
Haggag Hassan Oddoul *Nights of Musk*
Mona Prince *So You May See*
Mohamed Mansi Qandil *Moon over Samarqand*
Abd al-Hakim Qasim *Rites of Assent*
Somaya Ramadan *Leaves of Narcissus*
Mekkawi Said *Cairo Swan Song*
Ghada Samman *The Night of the First Billion*
Mahdi Issa al-Saqr *East Winds, West Winds*
Rafik Schami *The Calligrapher's Secret • Damascus Nights*
The Dark Side of Love
Habib Selmi *The Scents of Marie-Claire*
Khairy Shalaby *The Hashish Waiter • The Lodging House*
The Time-Travels of the Man Who Sold Pickles and Sweets
Miral al-Tahawy *Blue Aubergine • Gazelle Tracks • The Tent*
Bahaa Taher *As Doha Said • Love in Exile*
Fuad al-Takarli *The Long Way Back*
Zakaria Tamer *The Hedgehog*
M.M. Tawfik *Murder in the Tower of Happiness*
Mahmoud Al-Wardani *Heads Ripe for Plucking*
Amina Zaydan *Red Wine*
Latifa al-Zayyat *The Open Door*